Max's Story

A Dog's Purpose Puppy Tale

Max's Story

A Dog's Purpose Puppy Tale

W. Bruce Cameron

Illustrations by
Richard Cowdrey

STARSCAPE

A Tom Doherty Associates Book
New York

MAX'S STORY: A DOG'S PURPOSE PUPPY TALE

Copyright © 2018 by W. Bruce Cameron

Reading and Activity Guide copyright © 2018 by Tor Books

Illustrations © 2018 by Richard Cowdrey

All rights reserved.

A Starscape Book
Published by Tom Doherty Associates
175 Fifth Avenue
New York, NY 10010

www.tor-forge.com

The Library of Congress Cataloging-in-Publication Data
is available upon request.

ISBN 978-0-7653-9501-6 (hardcover)
ISBN 978-0-7653-9503-0 (ebook)

Our books may be purchased in bulk for promotional, educational, or business use.
Please contact your local bookseller or the Macmillan Corporate and Premium
Sales Department at 1-800-221-7945, extension 5442, or by email
at MacmillanSpecialMarkets@macmillan.com.

First Edition: July 2018

Printed in the United States of America

0 9 8 7 6 5 4

For Evie Michon,
who has been in my corner
since before I even had a corner.

Max's Story

A Dog's Purpose Puppy Tale

1

The first thing I remember is a place of barking dogs.

That sound never went away. Sometimes loud, sometimes soft. Sometimes angry, sometimes panicky, mostly just a loud call for attention. "I am here!" the barking said, over and over and over. "I am here! Notice me!"

When I could open my eyes, I learned that my mother was a light brown color. My two siblings were the same. All three of us squirmed toward our mother's fur and her warmth. We found her milk and drank, then we curled together and slept, then we woke to drink again.

Sometimes I heard a sound that was different from the barking. Voices. The voices belonged to women, I realized. I couldn't understand their words, but the sounds were gentle.

"Good dog," they said. "Good dog, Zoey."

I wondered if my mother's name was Zoey. I wondered if I had a name as well.

Even though the voices were soft, my mother trembled when they came near. I could feel her shivering as I cuddled close against her.

One day I blinked my eyes open when I heard one of the voices. I peered up. And up. And up. Then I stared in surprise.

The person saying "Good dog" in such a gentle voice was a giant! She loomed far above us. Her head blocked the light.

"Such cuties," she said.

A hand reached down to stroke my mother from her ears all along her back. I cringed, huddling deeper into my mother's warm fur. That hand was bigger than I was!

I did not want these giants touching me.

As my sisters and I got older, we began to leave our mother's side more often. But there was not far for us to go. In every direction, we were surrounded by walls made of chilly metal wire. I bit the wire a few times, but it did not taste good and it hurt my teeth. I wandered back to my mother, who licked my head. Then a sister thumped into me and stepped on my face.

When the giants came to the door of our cage, my sisters ran over to them, wagging their tails so hard that their entire bodies wobbled. Sometimes they even fell over! But I hung back behind my mother while the two girls got petted and sometimes even scooped up in those huge hands. They would lick the women's great big faces and yip in happy voices.

Why weren't they afraid?

One day a woman reached her hand all the way into the cage for me and hoisted me up into the air. Her fingers closed around me, holding me firmly, as she lifted me.

I did not like it. I growled at her.

"Hello, Max," she said. "You're pretty brave, huh? You going to be a watchdog?"

Another woman came up to peer at me. I growled at her, too. "I'm thinking father was a Yorkie, maybe?" she said. "Don't you think so, Gail?"

"Sure looks like a Chihuahua-Yorkie mix," the one holding me agreed. "He thinks he's tough. He's got a lot to learn!"

Gail put me back into the cage with my mother, and I backed away in a hurry.

My sisters' names, I learned, were Abby and Annie. Every now and then the three of us were taken to another room and put into a pen with some other dogs. Like the people, they were giants. But they were still young, just puppies, like we were.

I could tell because they ran clumsily, sometimes tripping over their own paws. They barked with excitement all the time. And they didn't know that it isn't polite to race up to another dog and sniff his face and jump up to put your paws on his head before you've even been introduced.

I'm not sure how I knew that this isn't the way to go about it, but somehow I did. I darted sideways as a young dog with black fuzzy fur came lolloping up to me, trying to show him that the proper way to meet a new dog is to sniff under the tail first. *Then* comes the chasing and wrestling.

He shoved his nose beneath my rear legs and lifted me off my feet, dumping me in a heap.

I jumped up and shook myself, ready to growl, but he was already running away. Irritated, I took myself to the edge of the pen. On the outside, a huge white dog lowered his nose to sniff at me. His head was bigger than my mother's whole body!

I backed up, barking, to show him that I wasn't scared.

And that's when I realized an important truth. All of the dogs around me and the women who took care of us—they weren't big. It was the other way around. *I* was small!

In fact, I was tiny!

It was such an astonishing thought that I sat still, stunned, until the same black dog who had shoved me so rudely before came galloping up and knocked me right over.

He put a paw on my chest, pinning me down. I thrashed my legs and shook my head. He was heavy! I wanted him off me!

He panted down at me, and I'd had enough. I growled. I showed him all of my teeth. And I barked as loudly as I could, right into his face.

He leaped back with a startled yelp, and I was free. I scrambled to my feet. But I wasn't done yet.

Maybe I was small, but that didn't mean it was all right for other dogs to pin me down. Right then and there, I decided that *I* was the one who should be in charge. I didn't lie down on my back and tuck my tail under for anybody!

I kept my lips back from my teeth to show the other puppy that I meant business. I walked slowly toward him. Somehow I knew to make my legs stiff so I'd be as tall as I possibly could. I lowered my head and felt the fur along my spine bristle, even though I hadn't told it to.

The other dog backed up a few more steps. Then he flopped down meekly and lay on his back, showing me his stomach and throat.

I stood over him for a moment so he'd be sure to get the message, and then I let him get up.

Maybe I was small, but it didn't mean I could be pushed around. I'd have to work very hard to let other dogs know that I was the one in charge.

People, too. People with their giant hands and their loud voices—I'd have to show them that they could not simply do whatever they wanted with me. It was important, I realized, as I looked around the pen where the other puppies were running and chasing and wrestling and barking. A few had curled up for quick naps.

I had to show the world that I mattered because there was something I had to do. A job. I had a job. I don't know how I knew, but I did. The knowledge was part of me, deep inside, just like I'd known to drop my head and show that other puppy my teeth to make him back down.

There was somebody I was supposed to take care

of. A girl. A human girl. She was somewhere out there in the world, and she needed me.

I'd find her soon. I wasn't sure how, but I would. And once I found her, I'd protect her.

To do that, I'd need to be the toughest, strongest, fiercest dog I could be. No matter what size I was.

My sisters and I went into the pen with other puppies again and again, and every time I showed them all that I was in charge. They learned pretty quickly. I didn't have to snap very often. I could tell them with the way I walked, my head up, my ears forward, my tail high. I could tell them with my voice, which was becoming louder and louder, and every now and then by showing my sharp little teeth.

"Be nice, Max," Gail would say. Yes. That was me. My name was Max, and I was a dog to be reckoned with.

After a while, my mother's milk was not enough to keep my stomach filled, and the women began to bring bowls of soft food to our cage. Abby and Annie learned to let me eat first. And then came a day when we were picked up and taken out of our cages with leashes clipped to our collars.

The cage door shut, leaving our mother behind.

My sisters looked back and whimpered. I wasn't sure why they did it, but I knew that something did feel different this time.

"Let's go," said the woman. "Time to find you guys a home."

Our mother pressed herself against the cage door and whined gently, once. Then she simply watched as we were led away.

We didn't go to the pen with the other puppies as we usually did. Instead, we were taken outside to a car and put into a large wire cage in the back. When I heard a deep, low hum, it startled me so much that I barked. Then the car started to shake and quiver around us!

My sisters were frightened and huddled against me. I sat bolt upright, alert, watching carefully in case this new sound and vibration turned out to be something I should fight. That's when I understood that we were moving. Through the windows I could see trees and buildings and sky and clouds pass by. We were going somewhere!

The place we were going turned out to be a park.

A park, I learned, was trees and bushes, grass and sky, and people. Lots of people. Gail scooped me up; I growled a little, just to let her know that I wasn't helpless, that I was allowing her to carry me. She took me to a new pen and set me down inside it.

For the first time I felt grass under my paws. It was odd, soft and prickly at once. And the smells! They rushed over me like a tidal wave. I didn't even bother to raise my hackles or lift my lips over my teeth to make sure the other puppies in the pen understood that I was the boss. I just stood with my nose lifted to the air, drinking it all in.

Warm dirt. A soft green smell with a little sharpness to it, that was the grass I stood on and the leaves all around. Something choking and dirty that came from other cars like the one that had brought us here, rushing past not far away. The cool smell of water, more of it than came in our bowls. And food! Food everywhere! Great gusts of food smells swirling all around me.

And people. This place carried the scent of people, more people than I had ever smelled in my entire life.

2

In the park, I found out that people just weren't giving me the respect I felt I deserved.

Gail and the others at the shelter were not too bad. I was used to them, and I'd gotten to the point where I didn't mind their gigantic hands reaching down to pet me—at least not most of the time. They picked me up carefully, so I put up with it. They spoke softly and their voices were gentle.

The people in the park were not always like that.

They crowded around the pen and talked loudly. Some of them—the smallest ones—squealed in high voices that sounded like my sisters when they got excited. Hands reached down, grabbing at me—so many hands! I stayed back, out of their reach. The right person, I was sure, would not grab or snatch. The right person would treat me with kindness.

Abby and Annie, though, rushed over to the fence to meet the people. Many of the other puppies did as well. They licked the hands that reached for them and squirmed happily as they were picked up. The people laughed. Everyone seemed happy, dogs and people alike.

I was not interested. I knew, deep down, that none of these people was right for me. But when Gail put her hand down into the pen with something in it that smelled enticing, my ears perked up.

"Come on, Max," she coaxed. "Come here."

That smell—it leaked out from her hand, and it made my mouth water. What *was* it? My mouth felt full of saliva, and my tongue slipped out between my teeth. I started toward her hand. She kept it still and let me pick something tiny and delicious from between her fingers. A treat!

"Good boy," she said softly.

She scratched under my chin, and I allowed her to do it. But when another hand came down, smelling of soap and harsh smoke and sweat, I jerked back, startled. A growl slipped out, and the fur on my back bristled.

The hand pulled away.

"Pretty aggressive for such a little thing," a voice said. The man standing near Gail shook his head. "I have kids at home—we can't have an aggressive dog. Don't you have any who are more mellow?"

Gail nodded as I backed away farther, and she called to my sister. The man scooped Abby up in his hands and laughed.

"Perfect! My kids will be so happy. Thanks! Is there paperwork to fill out?"

"At that table over there," Gail said, and the man carried Abby away.

A few minutes later, a giggling boy reached into the pen to pick up Annie and held her close to his face. Annie licked the boy's chin and nose with delight, and that was the last time I ever saw either of my sisters.

More and more puppies were taken out of the pen as the afternoon wore on. Sometimes Gail would call me over to the fence for another treat, but her hand was the only one I allowed to touch me.

"Mommy! Puppies!" a high-pitched voice shrieked.

A girl rushed over to the pen, curly dark hair

bouncing on her head. She nearly fell over the fence as she reached in, her small, soft hand darting straight at my face.

Instinctively, I snapped. My teeth clamped shut an inch from her fingers. It was just a warning, meant to make her back off, as it did for the other puppies. But she shrieked as though I'd actually bitten her, and a tall woman standing behind her snatched her up with a gasp.

"Max! No!" Gail scolded, and I backed away. "I'm so sorry. I think she startled him," she told the lady holding the girl.

"You shouldn't bring a dog like that to the park!" the woman said indignantly, hugging the little girl close. "It's all right, sweetie. That mean dog can't get you now."

Gail sighed as the woman carried the girl away. I was relieved. The girl had gotten the message that she couldn't just pet me or grab me whenever she liked. I'd have to be sure all the people learned the same thing.

As the afternoon wore on, most of the other puppies left with one person after another. At last there was only me.

A man came to join Gail at the fence. "Nobody interested in Max today?" he asked her.

"'Fraid not," she answered with a sigh. "He nipped at a little girl this morning."

The man shook his head. "Even if we did adopt him out, I'm not sure anybody would be able to handle him," he said.

"We don't know that. If someone can train him, really take the time . . . He might be fine. I think Max is one of those dogs who could really bond with the right person."

"Well, he might get lucky next week," the man said. "One more event. Then we'll have to put him on the list. I'm sorry, Gail, but you know that's how it goes."

"I know. Poor Max." Gail's voice was sad, but I didn't pay much attention to that. Something had caught my eye, and I moved to the side of the pen so I could see more clearly.

It was a girl.

She was older than the little one I'd had to warn away, but not as old as Gail. Sort of in between. She was walking slowly down a pathway of the park, holding three dogs on leashes. One was enormous, the largest I'd ever seen, a black-and-white mountain of a dog loping easily along. The other two were smaller, one black and curly all over, the other with short, light brown fur.

But I was not as interested in the dogs as I was in the girl. There was something about her. Her hair swung loose to her shoulders, bouncing a little with her steps. The wind shifted a little and brought her scent to me, and I smelled sweat, and shampoo, and something minty that she was chewing, and nervousness, and loneliness, and something else, something that was just *her*.

And I knew. This girl was mine. The one I had been waiting for.

I threw myself against the fence, barking and barking. I jumped up and scrabbled at the cold wire with my paws, but it was much too high for me to get out. I shook my head in frustration and ran in a frantic circle, barking and barking, trying to make her hear me.

If she heard me, she'd understand. She'd come and get me. She'd reach into the pen and pick me up, and I wouldn't snap, not at her. She'd take me away like the people had taken my sisters and the other puppies, and we'd be together.

Because that was why we were here, I realized. Dogs were supposed to be with humans. All the other puppies in the pen had found the right people, and I had to do the same.

But this girl, the right girl, somehow didn't hear

me. My barks were not loud enough to reach her. I was not big enough to jump the fence and race to her. She walked steadily on with the three dogs on the leashes, and Gail reached down into the pen.

"My goodness, Max, what is all the racket about?" she asked, lifting me up. "Careful, now! You'll make me drop you!"

I wiggled and whined in her hands, frustrated and unhappy. She needed to let me down! I had to chase after that girl!

But Gail carried me back to the car and popped me inside a small pen in the back, and my last chance to find the girl was gone.

T he next week I was put in the car again and taken back to the park. This time Gail didn't put me in the pen with the other puppies. She took me to a smaller pen where I could be by myself.

"Maybe you'll be more comfortable on your own," she said. "Don't worry, Max. You'll find a home. But be nice, okay? Be nice."

I looked out past the wire of the pen, wondering about the girl. *My* girl. I'd seen her here before. Would she be back this time? I had to be ready. If she came, I had to be sure that she'd see me.

Three times people came to my pen and reached their hands down inside it. None of these hands belonged to the girl, so I slunk away and growled. Each time the hands drew back.

"What happened? Was he abused?" a man asked Gail.

"No, he was born in the shelter. I don't know. Max is just . . . not that friendly. He doesn't play well with other dogs, either. He needs to find the right person. I think he'd do well with someone who stays at home and doesn't get many visitors."

"Well, that's not me!" the man said, laughing. He went over to the pen with the other dogs and I saw him scoop up a white puppy with eyes that were nearly invisible in puffs of fuzzy fur.

Then I looked away and saw *her*.

She did not have the other dogs with her this time. She was by herself, wearing a backpack, walking quickly, looking down at the ground.

I yipped. She kept walking.

I barked louder. I clawed at the wire of my pen. She had to notice me this time! I barked even louder, making it a command. It was the kind of bark that made even the grown-up dogs at the shelter take a step back from me.

And it worked. The girl looked up, and her head swung around. She saw me.

She paused. She smiled. And she came over to my pen.

Everything was all right! She'd found me!

The girl knelt down. She put her fingers through the wire and rubbed my ears gently. She chuckled.

"Hey, there, tiny thing," she said. "You've got a big bark for such a little guy."

I let her scratch my neck for a minute. She was very good at it. Her fingers knew just the right spots.

"Oh, be careful!" said a voice from behind her. "That's Max. He's . . ."

Gail's words trailed off as the girl scratched harder and I leaned against her hand.

"Aggressive," Gail finished. "Huh. He seems to like you a lot."

"He's sweet," the girl said.

"Believe me, nobody has ever called Max sweet before. Are you interested in adopting a dog?"

The girl looked up. "Oh, I wish I could. But I already have a dog. I mean, not now . . . I don't have her right now . . . I mean, I'm just in New York for the summer. My dog's at home. I'm sorry."

She'd stopped scratching. I licked at her fingers

to remind her to start again—or maybe to reach into the pen and get me so we could be together.

But for some reason the girl didn't seem to understand. She pulled her hand away and stood up.

"Sorry. I wish I could," she said to Gail.

"I wish you could, too," Gail answered.

The girl sighed. "I have to go," she muttered.

And then she left.

She walked away!

My girl was leaving without me!

3

I whined and scratched at the wire of the pen. I barked to let the girl know she'd made a mistake. But she didn't turn around. She just pushed her hands into her pockets and walked faster.

Gail sighed. She pulled a leash out of her pocket and reached down into my pen.

"I'm sorry, Max," she said sadly. "So, so sorry. But it looks like this just isn't going to work out."

She clipped the leash onto my collar and picked me up. That's when I saw my chance.

I snapped, my teeth closing so close to Gail's fingers that I could almost taste her skin. She gasped and her grip on me loosened. One squirm, one push with my back legs, and I was free!

I was also falling.

I thumped to the ground and staggered. Gail dropped to her knees and grabbed for my collar. But I didn't let her touch me. I got my balance back, and then I leaped and dodged and ran as fast as I could, the leash trailing behind me.

I had to get to my girl!

I jumped off the grass and onto a winding path. My girl had gone this way and I had to follow.

There were feet all around me—some in sandals, some in sneakers, some in shiny shoes with high heels. One pair of feet was even in shoes with wheels! Those zipped past me so quickly that the wind they made ruffled my fur and made my ears twitch.

Some of the feet jumped aside as I ran past. Others stood still and I darted around them. "Catch him!" I heard Gail's voice call faintly behind me. But I ran on.

Huge wheels three times as tall as I was whizzed past me—a person on a bike. I swerved to one side, off the path and onto the grass. "Watch out!" I heard the rider shout, and the bike wobbled. I heard something crash to the asphalt, but I didn't look back to see what had happened. I was running again.

The grass was easier to run on, I discovered—softer for my paws and with fewer feet to dodge. But up ahead there was one set of feet, and I was rapidly getting closer to them.

Just as I got ready to dart around the feet, something huge and blue and wiggly came down from above. Long tubes of bright color, twisted together, wobbled and jiggled in the breeze. It smelled dreadful—a rubbery, unnatural smell. "Want a balloon animal, little pup?" rumbled a voice.

I skidded to a stop, stiff-legged. I growled, my fur bristling.

The man holding the threatening object shook it at me and laughed. "Just a doggy like you!" he said.

The thing lurched at my face. I lunged forward and bit. This time it was not a warning—I meant it. This thing was attacking me!

My sharp teeth made contact. That would teach this dreadful thing to stay away from me!

A deafening bang exploded in my ears, and my legs took off running in spite of me. I would never run away from another dog, but this thing wasn't a dog. It was horrible!

Without planning to, I dashed under some bushes and squirmed beneath their lowest branches. I was small enough to do this without even slowing down—at least not much. When I burst out again, I was on a sidewalk. Straight in front of me was a street, and crossing the street—there she was! My girl!

Her back was to me. She couldn't hear me bark. But I was so close to her now! I raced across the sidewalk and, without slowing down for a second, sailed off the curb.

Now instead of feet, I was surrounded by tires, all of them motionless. They were much bigger than I was and smelled a little like that terrifying blue thing back in the park, but worse. A dirty, burned smell choked my nose as I ran.

When I was halfway across the street, the tires started moving.

"Watch out for that dog!" somebody shouted.

A tire was coming right at me! I was faster than it was, though, and I scooted out of the way, ducking underneath a heavy truck.

I was beginning to pant, and the air on the street tasted as bad as it smelled. But I forced my legs to move as quickly as possible—I had to!—and I darted out from under the truck before it could pick up too much speed. Another curb was right ahead.

Then something yanked at my neck. My leash! I flopped back onto my hind legs as one of the tires behind me drove over the leash, holding me back.

In a moment the tire rolled on, though, and I was free. I heaved my front paws up on the curb, scrabbled at the concrete with my claws, and crawled up on shaking legs. My throat ached where the leash had pulled so hard on my collar. I stood, trembling from my wild run and panting for breath.

I looked around for my girl.

There she was, not twenty feet away from me! She'd left the sidewalk and turned down a smaller walkway that led to the front door of a tall building. Two glass panels in the wall slid open right where she was standing.

I was so tired, but I knew I had to catch up. I forced myself into a dead run again. The drag from the leash slowed me down a little, but I pushed myself to keep moving. I raced down the walkway after my girl, too out of breath even to bark.

She stepped inside the building. The glass doors slid shut behind her.

Frantically, I threw myself against the doors. I gasped in a big breath and barked as loudly as I could.

The doors did not open for me. They stayed shut, and my girl could not hear me.

Footsteps came up behind me. "Hey, little dog, where do you belong?" said a voice.

I glanced up to see a man in a yellow shirt standing there. He was reaching down and I thought I'd have to show him, just like I'd shown all those people in the park, that I was Max—not a dog to be picked up by just anybody. But before I could do it, the glass doors in front of me suddenly slid open.

I tore inside, looking for my girl.

The floor was slick under my feet. I skittered and slid, my claws spread wide, and looked around frantically.

Then I saw her. She was standing in a tiny room with a light on over her head. Her eyes went wide and her mouth fell open a little when she saw me.

In front of her, two doors started to inch shut, just as the glass doors had done before. I wasn't going to let that happen to me again!

I gripped the slippery floor hard with my claws, braced myself, and leaped in with her, jumping up to put my paws on her knees, sobbing for breath as the doors slid shut behind me.

"Oh no!" the girl gasped.

Suddenly my leash yanked hard on my neck for a second time, dragging me down to the floor. I let out a strangled yelp of surprise and pain.

"You're caught!" the girl cried out. She dropped to her knees. I pulled hard against the leash, trying to go to her, but something was steadily hauling me backward.

My mouth opened but no sound came out. My collar had cut off my air. I couldn't breathe.

"Oh no, no, no!" the girl whimpered. She grabbed hold of my collar, too. This wasn't helping! I gagged as she pulled on the collar in one direction and the leash pulled in the other.

Then, with a snap, the collar broke open in the girl's hands. My leash whipped back through the crack between the doors and vanished, and I flopped against the cool floor, breathing hard and shaking.

"Oh, puppy," the girl said, and her voice was shaking, too. "You could have been killed!" Very carefully, she picked me up and held me close to her chest. Her smell was all around me, comforting and soothing, and I felt better at once. I smelled other dogs on her skin and a new scent I hadn't met before—some kind of animal that I had never seen.

I licked at her face and neck to let her know that

I was okay. Everything was okay, now that we were together.

But I hoped she'd learned her lesson and wouldn't leave me behind again.

4

"You're that little puppy from the park, aren't you?" the girl said as she got to her feet, holding me in her arms, close to her face. I didn't really understand her words, but I was glad just to hear her voice.

I could hear kindness in it, and I could feel the same kindness in her hands and the careful way she held me. Kindness flowed out of her, surrounding me. It made me relax against her with a sigh. I'd known the right person for me would be kind, and now I was proven right.

She pushed a button on the wall and the little room seemed to shift and rumble. It was strange, but

I wasn't worried anymore. There was nothing to worry about now.

The doors slid open, and the man in the blue coat I'd seen outside was standing there. "Hey, CJ," he said. "Is that your dog? I wasn't sure who he belonged to."

The girl—I guessed her name was CJ—shook her head. "No, he's not mine. But he jumped into the elevator with me."

The man reached out a hand toward me, and I gave him a warning growl. I couldn't tell if he meant to touch me or CJ, but either way, he needed to watch out. Nobody was going to touch CJ, not when I was around.

The man pulled his hand back. "Spunky!" he said.

My name was Max, not Spunky. I ignored him.

"I think he came from the adoption event over in the park," the girl said. "I'll take him back."

She carried me outside and kept me secure in her arms as we crossed the street and headed back into the park. It was funny to be riding so high. Now, instead of feet and wheels, I could see faces. Most of them looked straight ahead, maybe frowning a little. Those belonged to people who walked quickly, as if they didn't have time to waste.

A few strolled more slowly, glancing around. Some of those looked at me in CJ's arms and smiled.

We passed by the man holding the dreadful bright-colored, rubbery things that had made such a loud noise earlier. I dug my whole head under CJ's arm to stay away from them. When I finally pulled my head out, the breeze wafted a familiar scent to my nose.

Dogs. Puppies, mostly. Their fur smelled like disinfectant and food and each other. The dogs from the shelter. I squirmed in CJ's arms and tucked my face into her neck. The shelter had not been a bad place, not really, not once I'd shown everyone that they needed to respect me. But it seemed strange to be going back that way, now that I had found my girl.

By this time I could hear the few puppies left in the pen barking away. "Um. Hi. Excuse me," CJ said. "I think this is one of your dogs?"

"It's Max!" Gail said from behind me. "Oh, thank goodness. I can't believe you found him! We've been looking all over the park!"

"He jumped right into an elevator with me," said CJ. "His leash got caught, and I was scared he was going to get strangled." She shuddered a little and I nuzzled her skin and licked at her ear. "He's adorable!" She stroked my back.

"That isn't what most people say about him," Gail said. I snuck a look over my shoulder at her and wagged my tail, letting her know that I was happy now. She could go back to taking care of all the other dogs.

"So anyway," CJ said. "Where do you want me to put him?"

"Honestly?" Gail said. "I don't want you to put him anywhere."

There was a little pause.

"I can't," CJ said sadly. I licked more of her ear so she'd remember I was there to take care of her. There was no need to be sad. "I know you're looking for homes for the dogs, and I wish I could," CJ went on. "But I already have a dog at home. Molly. She's the best."

"So you like dogs?"

"Well, sure." CJ laughed. "Who doesn't like dogs?"

"And Max obviously likes you. Listen, it's not fair of me to put pressure on you like this, but Max . . . he's a one-person dog. He's aggressive with everybody he meets, but not you."

"Aggressive? This little thing?" CJ looked down at me in astonishment.

"He growls. He tries to bite. He snapped at me this morning, and I'm the one who's been feeding him. It's so sad, but we're not able to keep a dog like that. Tomorrow we'll have to have him put to sleep."

CJ gasped. "That's horrible!"

Gail sighed. I could not understand why the two of them were so sad. Why didn't CJ put me down so I could run? Why didn't the two of us go and play in the grass? Why were she and Gail just standing there saying words that neither of them seemed to enjoy?

"Well, sure it is," Gail said. "It *is* horrible. I don't like it any more than you do. But we're full. We have new dogs coming in every day. If we kept every dog we can't find a home for, we could never take any new ones. And the truth is, we can't put in the time to train a dog like Max. But if he had an owner, someone who could really work with him, I'm sure he'd be a great little dog."

Gail reached out and petted me. I let her do so without challenge—as long as she didn't try to take me away from my girl, I was fine with anything. "Look," Gail continued intently. "Dogs sometimes choose their people. We don't know how they know, but they just *know*. And that's what I think has happened with you and Max."

CJ looked down at me. Her eyes were moist, and a tear trickled down her cheek. I licked it up. It tasted of salt.

"I've never seen him take to anyone like that," Gail said. "But if you can't save him, well, you can't. Sometimes that's how it goes."

She held out her hands.

"No," said CJ. She held me tighter. "No. I can't believe I'm doing this, but okay."

"You'll take him?" Gail looked delighted. "That's great. It's wonderful. We'll waive the fee, don't worry about that. I'm just glad he has a chance."

CJ was happy, too, even though she was feeling some fear underneath the joy. She didn't understand yet that I was here to protect her. But I'd find a way to show her.

Gail and CJ talked some more and then, finally, CJ left, still holding me. I was beginning to get a little restless, ready to be down and running in the grass. But I was patient. We walked back to the tall building and returned to the small room with the lights.

I looked around alertly, remembering how my leash had been grabbed last time, but nothing bad happened. We stood in that room while the walls trembled a little and a rumbling sound came to my ears. Then the doors slid open once more. To my surprise, a new hallway was outside.

How strange! CJ held me and we walked past several doors. I could smell different things behind each one—meat cooking, something sweet, smoke, another dog, a sharp smell like the disinfectant at the shelter. We stopped at one that smelled of the other animal I had already noticed on CJ's clothes.

CJ shifted me to one arm so that she could take out a key from her pocket, turned it in the door, and opened it. We went inside.

CJ shut the door and set me down. At last! I shook myself and bowed to stretch my legs and began to investigate this new place.

There was a soft carpet on the floor that was excellent for holding scents. I could smell the rubber of CJ's shoes and another person, too, who smelled flowery and powdery and soapy. She didn't seem to be here at the moment, but clearly she spent a lot of time here.

That animal smell was very strong, too. It was female—I could sense that—but I wasn't sure of much else about it. It was something strange. Something new.

I sniffed around a couch and a big, soft chair and then headed into another room with a lot of excellent food smells. There was a bowl on the floor with small, crunchy bits of food in it, and I stuck my nose into it happily.

CJ snatched it away from me. "Max, no!" she said.

"That's Sneakers's food." I stood, looking up at her, and barked to tell her to put the food back down. After everything I'd gone through that morning, I was hungry!

"Well, okay," CJ said. "But I don't think you'd better get used to eating out of Sneakers's bowl." She opened a cupboard, took out another different bowl, this one white, and poured some of the food into it. Then she set it down on the floor for me.

I was pleased that CJ had gotten my message, and I ate the food quickly. There was water in another bowl, and I drank some of that. Then I was ready for more exploring.

Just as I was headed back out of the kitchen, a waft of scent fell over me. The creature that I had been smelling was here! I looked up and saw the new animal sitting in the center of the carpet, staring at me with narrow yellow eyes in a sleek gray face.

She was about my size, but I knew she was not a dog. The smell was wrong, and the face was, too. Pointy ears stood up on her head, but when I came closer she got to all four feet and put those ears back flat against her head. Her whiskers swept back against her cheeks.

Whatever she was, she needed to learn that I was

Max. I stood as tall as I could and walked confidently toward her. She would back down. They all did.

"Max, be good," CJ said. "That's Sneakers. Sneakers, it's okay. Be a nice cat. Max is going to live here now."

Sneakers the cat took a step back from me. That was right. She was learning.

Then Sneakers drew back her lips, showing teeth as sharp as mine, and let out a low, deep hiss. I was so startled that I jumped away. What kind of a noise was that for an animal to make? Why didn't she bark or growl or whine?

I recovered from my surprise, ready to show Sneakers that I couldn't be scared by a sound, but she crouched down and, in one movement, leaped to a tall counter between the kitchen and the living room. From high above, she looked down at me smugly as I stared up at her in astonishment. Then I raced into the kitchen and put my front paws up on the cabinets to bark as loud as I could.

This was completely unfair! How was I supposed to show this cat who was in charge when she could get up so high, out of my reach in an instant? I was so frustrated I ran in a small circle, and CJ laughed and scooped me up.

She took me into another room with a bed in it and plopped me down onto a soft blue quilt. I liked it. It smelled like her. She petted me and scratched my neck in that excellent way she had, and I sighed with contentment and curled up right next to her hand.

Then the door to the apartment opened and shut. "CJ? Are you here?" a loud voice called out.

I felt CJ go tense all over. I jerked my head up quickly. Was there something bothering my girl? Did I need to protect her?

"Okay, Max," she whispered. "Here we go. Be good, now. Please be good."

She picked me up and carried me out into the living room. A woman stood inside the door. I recognized her scent at once. She was the other person who lived here.

Her face was pale and her smooth dark hair just touched her coat's collar, which was gray and furry and smelled very intriguing. My nose twitched as she stared at us.

"Hi, Jillian," said CJ.

"What is *that*?" said the woman.

CJ took a deep breath. "This is Max."

CJ and the woman talked a lot. After a while CJ put me down so I could move freely. I stayed close to her feet, since I could tell she was not very happy.

"Look, your mother and I have been friends for a long time, and that's why I said you could stay here for the summer. But I didn't mean you could show up with an entire zoo!" Jillian said.

"It's *not* a zoo. It's just one dog. Look at him. He's so little. You won't even know he's here."

"I'm pretty sure I'll know. This is an apartment, CJ! A New York apartment! It's no place for a dog. What about—you know what I mean—calls of nature?"

"I'll take care of all that. I promise. And I'll feed him and walk him."

"And what about Sneakers? What if it chases her? Or bites her?"

"Sneakers is bigger than Max! And she already jumped up on the counter when he growled at her."

"He growled at her?"

"He didn't really mean it. It's just an act. I can tell. He's not really fierce. The people at the shelter were going to put him to sleep! Tomorrow! What if it was Sneakers? Wouldn't you want somebody to help her?"

Jillian sighed. She flopped down on the couch and ran both hands through her hair, fluffing it up and then smoothing it back from her face. "Well, it's *not* Sneakers. It's not a nice, clean, quiet cat who uses a litter box. It's a dog. How could you bring a dog into my apartment without telling me?"

"It was an emergency," CJ said, and her voice sounded so sad I sat down on her feet so I could be as close as possible to her. She bent to scoop me up in her hands.

"Please, Jillian. Let me keep him."

She brought her head down close to mine.

"Listen, Max," she whispered. "Be nice to her. It's your only chance."

CJ went to sit on the sofa beside Jillian, holding me in her lap. Her hands were snug around me.

"He's so cute, Jillian. And he's even smaller than Sneakers. Please let him stay."

Jillian sighed. She frowned. She looked at me.

Then she poked her fingers toward me rather awkwardly. I felt a growl rising in my throat, but CJ squeezed me a little tighter, and Jillian pulled her hand back before I needed to show her to watch her step around me.

I felt CJ relax. I sighed and flopped down in her lap, too. Apparently, Jillian was no threat to either of us. And I was tired and ready for a nap. It had been a very long day already.

"Oh, all right, I guess," Jillian said. "I guess I can put up with a dog for the summer. But I'm taking you at your word, CJ. I can't get complaints from my neighbors about barking, or come home to a mess.

And that thing can't bother Sneakers. Do we have a deal?"

"We do! We really do! I'll take care of everything. Don't worry!" CJ's voice spiked with happiness.

"If anything happens to my carpet, I might change my mind," Jillian muttered. "But okay, I guess. For now."

5

Before long, Jillian picked herself up from the couch. "I better make some dinner," she said. Sneakers jumped down from the counter and went to rub up against Jillian's ankles. Jillian swept the cat up and held her so that Sneakers's head tucked right under her chin.

Sneakers seemed to give me a taunting look from her perch. Then she closed her eyes to rub her head against Jillian's jaw. Unfair again. But the time would come when this cat would learn that I was the boss and she was not.

Jillian carried Sneakers into another room. Then she came out and went back into the kitchen while

CJ cuddled me on the couch. When Jillian came out again, she had a bowl full of cereal and a spoon.

Picking up something flat and rectangular, she pointed it at a screen on the wall. The screen erupted with color and sound and I twitched a little in CJ's lap. Was this a new threat I needed to protect her from?

"It's okay, Max. The TV won't hurt you," CJ said. Her hands stroked me soothingly, one on each side of my body.

"Get yourself something to eat," Jillian said, settling down into a chair across from the loud screen.

CJ set me on the floor and went into the kitchen, too. I stretched and thought I might go and see what had happened to Sneakers, but interesting smells drifted to my nose—bread, something sharp and spicy, meat! I hurried to see what CJ was doing.

She was putting meat between two slices of bread and spreading that spicy stuff on top of it. I whined at her feet. "You want some sandwich, Max?" she asked.

Whatever a sandwich was, I definitely wanted some!

CJ put some bits of her sandwich filling on a paper towel and set the whole thing down on the floor for me. I gobbled the meat up. Salty and delicious! Then

I gulped down more water from the bowl on the floor, which CJ refilled.

As CJ finished her half of the sandwich, I felt a familiar need and sniffed around the kitchen for the best spot to take care of it.

"Max! No!" CJ gasped as I squatted down in a corner.

I knew she was worried, but I couldn't stop what I was doing. As soon as I was done, I leaped alertly to her side, looking around for whatever had her anxious.

"Oh, Max, no," CJ said again. She picked up some paper towels and wiped up the puddle I'd just left.

"CJ, I warned you," Jillian said crossly, not moving from her chair.

"I'll clean it up. I'm sorry."

"This is why dogs don't belong in an apartment. Cats are really the only pets that work in a big city like New York."

"I'll take him out right now. I promise." CJ threw the paper towels in the trash. "Come on, Max!"

Her intent was clear, but actually I wasn't ready to "come on." I hadn't quite finished. But CJ seemed so urgent that I went with her, and I waited until I was outside to squat on the sidewalk and leave a little brown pile there.

"Good boy, Max. Good boy!" CJ said happily. She seemed so pleased that I wagged up into her face and panted happily. If my girl was happy, I was happy. It had been such hard work to find her, but together, we'd both be fine.

That night CJ sat on her bed and lifted me up to sit with her. She took a black rectangular thing from a table beside the bed. I'd learn later that people called these things phones and spent a lot of time looking at them that would be better spent with dogs, but that was the first time I'd seen one. I thought it might be something for me to play with and jumped forward, ready to wrestle it out of her hand.

"No, Max, not a toy!" CJ said, pushing me back. "Hold still. Okay, sit just like that. That's perfect!" The black thing made a click. I barked at it.

Then CJ tapped on the phone for a while, until I shoved my nose under her hand to remind her that I was the one who needed petting. "Okay, Max, okay," she said, scratching me behind the ears with that perfect touch she had. "I just wanted to send a picture of you to Trent."

The phone made an odd jangly noise. I jumped,

startled, and put my paw on it to teach it not to do that.

CJ pulled it away, looked at it for a moment, and laughed. "Trent says he should have known I couldn't make it all summer without finding a dog somewhere! Look, Max." She held the phone up in front of my face. I sniffed it. It did not smell particularly interesting.

"That's Molly," CJ told me. "She's my dog back home. Trent's taking care of her for the summer. He says she misses me."

Her voice sounded sad. Maybe the phone was making her sad. I nosed it out of her hand and stood right in front of her, jumping up to put my front paws on her chest and lick her chin.

"Oh, Max!" She laughed, which made me glad. I'd gotten the phone away from her, and now she was happy. That was one of my jobs, keeping my girl happy. And the other was to protect her from anything that might hurt her.

That night I slept in CJ's bed, curled up against the warmth of her body. It was perfect. And in the morning she took me out for a quick walk and bought a bag that smelled absolutely delicious. From it she poured me a bowl full of crunchy things that I gobbled up happily.

CJ had moved Sneakers's bowl up onto the counter, so that I couldn't get at the food it held. Sneakers was sitting up there now, eating and peering down haughtily at me. I ignored her. She just didn't understand how things worked in this apartment, but eventually she would learn.

Then CJ clipped my leash onto my collar again. "Come on, Max," she said.

Jillian came out of her room, wrapped in a fuzzy blue robe. "Up already?" she said sleepily.

"It's ten o'clock," CJ said. "I've got to get to work."

Jillian yawned. "Have fun."

It was wonderful being CJ's dog. So many walks!

CJ took me down the hall to the same little room we had ridden in yesterday. (I found out later it was called the elevator.) While we were waiting for the doors to open, I lifted my nose. A remarkable smell was drifting down the hallway.

Another dog. Male. Big. Angry. "Whoa, hold on, Baxter!" said a man's voice, and I heard CJ's breath draw in quickly and felt her worry spike.

She didn't need to worry. I was here to take care of her. I looked the same way she was looking and saw a brown-and-black dog with thick fur and alert, triangular ears that stood up high on his head. He was pulling hard on his owner's leash, yanking the man down the hall toward us.

I stood up straight, felt my hackles rise, and got ready to show this dog who was in charge. But CJ reached down and snatched me up. She started to back away.

I squirmed impatiently in her arms, pushing with my legs. How was I going to show Baxter who was the boss if I couldn't get close to him?

"What's that? A muff?" Baxter's owner laughed as they both came closer. Baxter showed me his teeth and CJ backed up farther.

"A Yorkie-Chihuahua mix," she said stiffly. "Can you hold on to Baxter, please?"

The man stopped about seven or eight feet away from us, pulling Baxter's leash. The collar went tight around his neck, cutting off his growl.

I squirmed harder, getting impatient for CJ to let me down so I could make it clear to Baxter that he had the wrong idea. My girl didn't understand how to treat a dog like that, though. She moved even farther away as the elevator dinged and the doors opened.

"Better keep that little toy out of Baxter's way," the man said, yanking the big dog onto the elevator.

"He wouldn't even make a good mouthful! You getting on or not?"

"We'll take the stairs," CJ said coldly. The doors shut on Baxter's barking as she carried me down the hallway. "Max, stay away from Baxter," she told me, opening a door that led to a staircase. "Most dogs are nice, but that one—even I don't like that one. I'm glad he never comes to the dog park."

After that CJ showed me how marvelous it was going to be to be her dog.

First we went to another apartment on the floor below Jillian's. When CJ knocked on the door, a woman opened it and there was a dog beside her, a leash trailing from his collar. CJ still had me in her arms, which meant this dog and I were just about eye to eye. Later I heard CJ call him a Great Dane.

I had seen him before, the first time I'd spotted CJ. He looked even bigger up close! His white coat was spotted all over with black blobs, each bigger than my whole body. He put a giant nose right into my face without even checking to see if it was all right. Then, to my astonishment, he put out an enormous tongue and lapped it over my face!

I shook my wet head indignantly and barked as loudly and fiercely as I could. I could smell that he didn't mean any harm, but still—he needed to be polite.

The big dog took a step or two back in surprise. His head and ears went down apologetically.

"Duke, you're such a big baby," his owner said, laughing. "Who's this?"

"This is Max," CJ said.

"He sure is cute," the woman said, and she reached out to rub my head. I showed my teeth. This woman smelled nice, like food—eggs and bacon!—and like Duke. But even so, I was CJ's dog, not hers.

She snatched her hand back. I was pleased she'd understood.

"Whoa! Kind of ferocious for such a little puffball. What's the deal? Why is he so aggressive?"

"I don't know." CJ hugged me tighter. "I'm working on it."

She set me down and took Duke's leash in her hand. The big dog came out with us into the hallway. He turned out to be all right, once he understood that I was going to lead the way.

We went out into the street and stopped at two different buildings to pick up the other two dogs I'd seen with CJ before. The first was a fuzzy black male with a puffball on his tail; the second was a tan female, old enough to walk slowly. The black poodle, Jay, bounced around me and barked with excitement, but I stood my ground and raised my hackles just a little. He seemed to understand that he shouldn't get carried away.

The female was named Honey. She sniffed me once, and then sat down with a sigh and looked at me. That seemed to mean she wasn't going to challenge me, any more than Duke or the poodle was. But somehow I couldn't quite get over the feeling that she was humoring me.

It didn't matter too much, however, because CJ took us all out onto the street again and there was so much—*so much!*—to see and smell that even bossing the other dogs fell to the back of my mind. She held my leash and Duke's in one hand, and Jay's and Honey's in the other. I pushed to the front of the pack, where I belonged, and led us all through the streets of New York.

So far, I had only known the shelter and the park and CJ's apartment. Sure, there had been that run through the streets while I chased CJ, but then I'd been so intent on catching up with my girl that I hadn't been able to enjoy myself.

Now every step brought fascinating new smells. The sidewalk smelled like feet, thousands of feet, each trail crossing and crisscrossing the others and going off in new directions. To our right, cars growled and grumbled as they swept by. On our left there were many doors that opened and closed. Each time, delicious scents wafted out—coffee, sugar, baking bread, sizzling oil, cooking meat.

Every corner brought us to tall trash cans filled with fascinating garbage. Jay thought he was going to be first to sniff, but I taught him differently with a quick snap at his front feet.

"Max! Don't be like that!" CJ said. I could tell she was worried, but I was too busy inhaling the scents of coffee in old paper cups to help her out right then. There were sandwich scraps inside the metal can and sugary liquid dripping down its sides. I let the other dogs sniff after I'd had my turn, and then CJ pulled us on.

My nose worked without stopping. Even more intriguing than all the food smells and all of the feet was the smell of many, many dogs.

Dogs had been here. Every garbage can, every streetlight, every fire hydrant told me about them. Big dogs, small dogs. Old ones and puppies. Sick and healthy, male and female, in a hurry or out for a leisurely stroll. They'd left their marks everywhere in this city. I left my own on top of theirs as often as CJ would let me.

That way they'd all know that I was Max, and I was here, and I was important.

CJ led us all to a gate and took us through onto a patch of worn-out grass and clawed-up dirt. I looked around with satisfaction.

There were dogs everywhere. A lot of them were the ones I'd smelled on the sidewalk. Dogs chasing, dogs running, dogs huddled by their owner's legs or prancing proudly across the ground. A park that was full of dogs, all of them ready to learn that I was Max.

6

CJ reached down to unsnap our leashes from our collars. I leaped forward with delight. This would be like the puppy pen back at the shelter, only bigger!

Jay yipped and tore past me, racing madly to the far corner of the park and then back again. Honey trotted away to touch noses and sniff rears with a few dogs she seemed to know, and then settled down with a sigh in the shade of a tree. Duke wandered along a few feet behind me.

A young brown dog with stiff, wiry fur came bounding up to me. I stood tall and put my ears forward, but she didn't get the message—she just stuck her nose right in my face. Then she jumped to my rear, shoving her muzzle beneath my tail so hard that I flopped forward onto my chin.

I leaped to my feet and spun around, ready to teach her better manners, but she was already bounding away. Frustrating!

I heard CJ laughing behind me and was glad that she was happy, but that didn't solve the problem of these dogs and their confusion over who was to be obeyed.

Duke ambled away, and I saw that he'd stuck his enormous muzzle into a big metal bowl of water that was sitting on the ground. A drink sounded good to me, too. It was a warm day and my tongue was already hanging. I hurried over and barked at Duke.

He stepped aside obediently.

The bowl was a little tall for me; I had to strain my neck to get over the rim. But the water was cool and delicious. I was lapping it up eagerly when the same wiry brown dog who had been so rude earlier came bounding up behind me.

I recognized her scent, but I didn't look around. She'd have to wait until I was done.

She still didn't seem to know about manners, though. She pushed her nose beneath my tail *again*, only this time she actually lifted my rear legs off the ground! Tipped off balance, I toppled forward. The entire front half of my body—nose, muzzle, head, and paws—ended up in the water dish.

I staggered back, shaking my head to get the water out of my eyes, jumping around to bark at the young female and teach her to behave, to keep her distance, to understand who I was! I was Max!

But she was already running away. I shook myself all over, sending water flying from my fur, and chased her. I'd show her!

I didn't get a chance, however, because a green, fuzzy ball bounced past my nose. My whole body snapped into alertness.

I'd seen balls before, at the shelter, but we hadn't had so much room to play there. The way this ball was bouncing and rolling over so much ground made a thrill of excitement rush through me. I wanted that ball. Now!

The trouble was, I wasn't the only dog who wanted that ball.

Three other dogs were after it, a sleek white one, a big brown-and-black one with pointy ears, and a yellow ball of fluff. But none of them was as close as me. I leaped after the ball, skidded, braced my feet, darted to the left as the ball hit a bump in the ground and bounced crazily, and got my teeth in it before all the other dogs made it there.

Or at least I *tried* to get my teeth in it.

That ball was almost the size of my skull! I opened my jaws as wide as I could, but I just couldn't get them to close around the curved surface. I tried nibbling at it, using just my front teeth, but it rolled away from me. Unfair!

The other three dogs came panting up, and the white one got low and snatched at the ball—at *my* ball! I jumped forward so that one front paw landed on either side of the ball. I pulled my lips back from my teeth. I felt the hair on my hackles bristling. My growls said that this was *my* ball. Mine! Mine!

The fluffy yellow dog backed away, but the white one didn't seem to get the message. He tried to snatch at my ball again, and I was forced to snap at his nose. And the big dog with the pointy ears had his eyes fixed on the ball, too, looking for any gap in my attention to grab it.

It was infuriating! That ball was *mine*!

I heard a *whuff* from behind me—not exactly a bark, but just breath rushing out of a dog's nose. And I caught a familiar scent. Duke was arriving. He'd better not have any ideas about grabbing my ball, either!

I turned back to look at him and saw the giant dog was closer than I'd realized, looming over me. My head barely reached halfway to his belly. He stood and wagged happily, his big face high above me. At least he seemed to have no plans to snatch my ball.

I returned my attention to the other two dogs and found that the white one was running away. The brown-and-black one looked at Duke for a moment and then turned, as if he'd heard his owner call. But I hadn't heard a thing.

It looked like the dogs in this park were starting to get the message, just like the dogs back at the shelter. I was Max. They'd better respect that. I kept a very careful eye on my ball until CJ came to clip my leash back on my collar. Then I led our pack all the way home.

It was nice to have some time to rest after such a busy morning. CJ made me a comfortable spot on the floor of her room with a soft towel to lie on, and I lay there and took a nap while she sat at a small desk and made scratching noises with a pencil on a big sheet of paper.

When I woke up, she was still doing the same thing. She had a frown on her face and was clutching the pencil tightly.

I got up, stretched, shook myself, and sniffed

around the room. CJ didn't even seem to notice that I was awake. I yawned and then squatted down near a corner of her desk.

CJ dropped her pencil. "Max! No!"

It was nice that she was paying attention to me again. It was less nice when she swept me up in her hands before I'd even gotten started! She rushed me out into the hall and held me as we waited for the elevator. It was a long wait and I was not in the mood! The minute we got outside, she set me down on the ground and I left a big puddle on the sidewalk.

"Good dog, Max. Good dog!" CJ crooned.

It was all very strange, but I loved it when she talked to me in that voice. I loved being a good dog for her.

We went back up to the apartment and CJ settled herself down at her desk again. I put a paw on her leg to remind her that dogs are more important than pieces of paper. Especially since the piece of paper didn't seem to be making her happy at all.

"I don't know, Max," CJ said in a low, frustrated voice. "I just don't know."

She bent down to pick me up. That was great. I settled into her lap and she scratched all around my neck.

"Maybe I'm not good enough," she said quietly

into my fur. "The other kids in this art program— they've had special lessons and art camps in the summer and all that stuff. One girl, she stopped by my table and looked at what I was doing. It was a picture of Molly. You'd like Molly, Max. She's the best dog ever. But this girl, she said, 'Oh, cute.' Cute! That's about the worst thing anybody can say."

I licked at her face. One cheek tasted a little salty, and when another tear slipped out of CJ's eye, I licked that up, too.

Her sadness and worry settled over us both. It was hard to understand why she was so miserable. I was here now, after all. We were together.

"Good dog, Max," she said, hugging me close. I snuggled my head into the skin of her neck, which smelled wonderful. But then she sighed and put me down on the floor and picked up her pencil again.

The door to her room opened.

"CJ? I'm going out for the evening," Jillian said. She stood in the hallway, wearing bright shoes with high, wobbly heels that made her look unsteady. "You're fine on your own, right?"

"Sure," CJ said, not looking up.

"Make yourself a sandwich or something for dinner."

"Okay."

Jillian took a step into the room. I watched with interest to see how she'd balance herself on those skinny heels. It looked like one little push would knock her right over.

A second step took Jillian a little too close to me. I pulled back my lip, ready to show my teeth and let her know to keep her distance. CJ looked up from her paper at last and noticed me. Her eyes widened.

"Jillian, what do you think of this?" she said a bit loudly, and made a flapping motion with her hand toward me. I was so surprised that my growl stopped in my throat. What did CJ want me to do?

I didn't understand, but at least Jillian stepped away from me, toward the desk, so I didn't have to warn her again.

"What is that even supposed to be?" she asked, peering over CJ's shoulder. CJ dropped her pencil.

"I don't know," she muttered.

"Seems like a lot of money your mom has to pay for an art program so you can draw something you can't even identify," Jillian said.

CJ picked up a big gray eraser and began scrubbing hard at her paper. "Gloria didn't pay. I got a scholarship. I'm walking dogs for my own spending money. Gloria doesn't have anything to do with this art program."

"Geez, okay." Jillian shook her head. "You seem really tense. Why don't you take a break? You've been working on that thing all afternoon. Go out and do something. It's not good for you just to hang around this apartment all the time."

CJ scrubbed harder at the paper. "I don't have anywhere to go."

Jillian stared. "Are you kidding? You're in the middle of the greatest city in the world! When I was your age, I was hardly ever home. My friends and I used to take the subway everywhere. Well, suit yourself. I'll be back around eleven." She tottered out.

"I don't have any friends, either," CJ muttered at her paper. But I didn't think Jillian could hear.

"No, Sneakers!" we heard Jillian shout from the living room. That sounded interesting, so I trotted out to see what might be happening.

Jillian was halfway through the door, which she'd opened just wide enough for her body. Sneakers was crouched at her feet, trying to find a way to wriggle past.

"No way, Sneakers. You stay in!" Jillian whisked herself all the way through the door and shut it. Sneakers sat in front of it and meowed loudly in frustration.

It seemed like a good time to remind Sneakers

who was in charge in the apartment. I stood up straight and headed for her, but she turned around and gave me a bored look.

I stood up taller. I walked toward her more slowly. I let my ears fall back a bit, to show her that I meant it.

Sneakers yawned. Yawned! Then she stood up and began slowly sauntering past me.

That was too much! I made a dash at her, and she jumped up onto the back of the couch, where she sat, licking her paw. I tried to jump up on the couch cushions, but they were too high for me, so I put my front feet up on them and barked loudly to let the cat know I had not forgotten her.

"Oh, Max, don't!" CJ suddenly scooped me up from behind. "If you're mean to Sneakers, Jillian might not let me keep you after all. Come on, let's go out for a bit. I'm not getting anything good done anyway."

CJ clipped my leash to my collar, dropped a few treats in a bowl for Sneakers, and left while that annoying cat was gobbling them up.

"Sneakers likes to sneak out," she told me as we walked to the elevator. "That's how she got her name."

I wasn't sure what she was saying, but I understood Sneakers's name. Probably she was telling me that I was a better pet than Sneakers.

I peed again once we got outside, even though I didn't have much to leave behind, just to hear CJ's delighted voice and feel her hands stroking me. Then we went for another walk down the sidewalk, me with my nose up high and twitching to take in all the fascinating smells on every side.

When we got to a street, CJ bent down to pick me up. "There's a lot of traffic, Max," she muttered. "I'll carry you."

She hesitated on the curb as cars whizzed past. When a break in the traffic came, she put a foot down into the street and then drew it back. She took a deep breath and stepped down again, walking out.

A horn blared and a voice yelled angry words. CJ jumped back to the safety of the curb, hugging me close, as a bright yellow car dashed past, so close the wind made my ears flap.

CJ's heart was beating quickly. I lapped at her chin to remind her that she was safe with me.

"Oh, Max," she said unhappily, low enough that only I could hear. "Sometimes I wish I could just go home."

7

CJ waited a long time on the curb, but we got across the street at last. Halfway down the next block, CJ tied my leash to a metal post that stuck up out of the ground and told me to wait for her. She went inside a store.

The post was interesting—lots of other dogs had been there and left their signs behind. It was too bad that my bladder was empty and I couldn't add my mark on top of theirs, where it belonged.

Feet walked past—some in tennis shoes, some in heavy boots, some in sandals. Most of them seemed in a hurry, although one or two pairs slowed down when they saw me. Once a big hand came down toward my head. I quickly let this stranger know that he was not the right person to pet me.

"Whoa! Mean little dog!" a voice said, and the hand very quickly went away.

It was all very interesting, but I was worried about CJ. Would she be all right inside that store without me to take care of her?

When she came back at last, she was carrying a bag in her hand. It smelled very good, and I tried to get up on my hind legs to get a better sniff.

"Later, Max," CJ said, untying my leash. "Come on, now. Let's go home."

Back at the apartment, she sat down on the floor in the living room and took a can out of the bag. She shook out something from the can into her hand. It had a smell that riveted my attention in two seconds—it smelled just like the treats Gail sometimes used to give me at the shelter.

But CJ closed her fist so I couldn't get at the treat. That was annoying. I nosed at her fingers and licked to let her know to open them up. Then, frustrated, I sat back and barked at her.

"No, Max," she said sternly. I was startled. Why was my girl talking to me like that?

"Gentle, Max," she said firmly. "Gentle."

I tilted my head to get a better view of her face and gazed at her, baffled.

"Good, Max. Good." She opened up her hand and let me have a treat. It was delicious! But it went down all too quickly. I wanted more.

She put another treat into her palm and closed her hand again. I barked and even let out a tiny growl of frustration, only to hear, "No, Max!"

What was going on?

"Gentle, Max," CJ said again. When I looked up at her, she opened up her hand and gave me another treat.

So "Gentle, Max" meant she'd give me something tasty? That was nice, I supposed. But it was still a strange game. Sneakers seemed to think so, too, because she came over to stare.

CJ was shaking another treat out of the can. An extra one fell to the ground, and Sneakers pounced.

That treat was *mine*! But it was hard to growl because I was still busy chewing the last one. Before I could really object, Sneakers had jumped up to the counter with my treat in her mouth. CJ laughed. I did not see what was funny, but she had more treats in her hand, and that was what was important, after all.

"Hmmmm," CJ said, looking from me to Sneakers. Then she let me have the treat in her hand and lick her fingers clean before going over to a little table next to the couch. She picked up a newspaper, which made an intriguing, rustling noise when she shook it. Sneakers and I both looked up.

"Come on, you two," CJ said, and she opened the door into the hall.

Sneakers's ears perked up and she leaped off the counter and shot through the door. I followed more slowly. After all, I knew that if CJ was going out into the hall, she'd probably take me with her. I didn't need to rush like a cat. I was Max, and I had dignity.

The hall stretched a long way in either direction. There might have been ten doors in each wall, with an elevator in the middle. Sneakers ranged up and down, sniffing at the carpet and the walls, her tail high and quivering with excitement. I stayed close to CJ, who sat down on the floor and ripped a long strip off the paper she'd brought with her.

My ears twitched. Sneakers's did, too, and she turned her head to look.

CJ crumpled up the paper into a ball, and then she took the can of treats out of her pocket. She stuffed one into the very center of the ball. Both Sneakers and I had our eyes riveted on the ball now.

"Get it!" she said, and she threw the ball as hard as she could down the hallway.

Sneakers sprang after the ball. It was not fair! She could jump such a long distance that she made it to the ball almost before I could get my feet moving.

She didn't seem to know what to do with the toy once she got it, though. Instead of putting it in her mouth, like any dog would, she put out a paw and batted it. The crumpled-up paper stuck to her claws, and she seemed startled and shook her paw as hard as she could, sending the ball flying.

That was my chance! I raced past her and seized the ball in my teeth. It wasn't like the green ball at the dog park; this one was the right size for my mouth. I shook my head hard, and the paper ripped, letting the treat fall out onto the carpet. I snatched it up before Sneakers could get it.

She didn't admit that I was in charge, however. Instead, she just turned her back on me, sat down, and started to wash one leg, as if she didn't even know I was there.

That wasn't what she should be doing! I meant to show her how things should be, but CJ, giggling, launched another rustling paper ball toward us.

Sneakers immediately stopped pretending that she didn't care and jumped toward it. Of course I had

to chase her, barking excitedly. She seized the ball in both front paws and for some strange reason flopped onto her back, bringing up her back paws to tear at the paper.

What an odd thing to do! It seemed as if she were showing me her belly and throat, giving in to me. But she had not let go of the ball with the treat inside it. Plus she had those back paws up in a threatening way.

What was going on, exactly?

I wanted to snatch the newspaper ball away from her, but her claws looked very sharp. I hesitated. She should obviously give the ball to me, since I was in charge. But how was I supposed to make it clear to her, since she didn't seem to understand?

"Here, Max!" CJ called. "Here's one for you!"

A ball of crumpled-up newspaper bopped me on the nose. I jumped back, barked at it in disapproval, then jumped on it to bite it hard. I'd show that ball! I'd show Sneakers how to tackle something like this!

Sneakers and I chased paper balls up and down the hallway and CJ laughed with delight. A few people even opened their apartment doors and peered out. When they saw what was going on, they smiled.

Finally Sneakers decided she was done. She sat down and began to lick one paw and rub it over her face. CJ collected all the chewed-up pieces of paper that we were done with.

"That's better, huh?" she said, bending down to stroke Sneakers's head. "Nobody should be cooped up in an apartment all the time."

Then she picked up Sneakers. How strange! Why would she do that? I sat at her feet and barked impatiently so that she'd remember I was her dog and pick me up instead.

"Come on, Max," she said, and opened the apartment door. I followed her and Sneakers back inside.

The next morning, CJ seemed in a big rush. She gulped down a bowl of cereal with milk and then ran around to shove pads of paper and pencil cases and markers into a backpack while Jillian sat in the living room, holding a steaming mug in her hand and looking at the TV. CJ took me outside to pee, but just as I was ready to head out for an interesting walk, she scooped me up and hurried back inside.

"Not now, Max! I'll be late!" she said as I squirmed in protest.

She dumped food and water in my bowls, and then she did something totally unexpected.

She ran out the door. She left. Without me!

I was so surprised that all I could think to do was sit next to the door and bark as loudly as I could, so that she'd realize her mistake and come back. But for some reason she didn't. It made no sense at all!

"Oh, be quiet!" Jillian said irritably. I looked over at her with impatience. She was no substitute for my girl.

Jillian put her coffee cup in the sink, wandered into her bedroom, and came out wearing different clothes. She settled down at a table in the living room and began to tap her fingers on a small plastic box while she frowned at a screen. The tapping made an interesting sound, and since CJ didn't seem to be coming back right away, I went over to sit at Jillian's feet to see if what she was doing had anything to do with me.

"Shoo," Jillian said, not looking down at me. This was not entertaining. I gave up and went back over to the door, waiting for CJ to return.

She did not return.

I waited some more.

Nothing happened.

I wandered into the kitchen and ate a few pieces of food that somehow remained in my bowl. Then I looked around for Sneakers's food, but it was still unfairly high up on a counter, where I could not get at it.

Perhaps, since there was nothing else to do, it was time that I taught Sneakers what it meant that I was her boss. Then maybe I'd get some of her food.

I sniffed and figured out that the cat was in the bedroom that CJ did not sleep in. The door was open a crack, so I nosed it wider and went in.

I had been right; Sneakers *was* there, curled up asleep on the bed, almost invisible in the midst of a soft, silky gray quilt. She didn't even twitch an ear when I entered.

I sat down and barked, so that she'd know I'd come into the room.

She lifted her head, gave me an irritated look out of her yellow eyes, and put her head back down. As if I didn't even matter! And the bed was too high. I could not get up on it at all.

I barked a little more, just to let her know how I felt.

"Quiet, little dog!" Jillian yelled from the other room.

Her voice was so different from CJ's. CJ's voice, when she talked to me, was gentle and kind and, most important, happy. I could tell she was glad just to be with me, the same way I was glad just to be with her.

But right now I *wasn't* with her. Where had she gone? Where were Duke and Jay and Honey, the pack I was responsible for? I was left in this apartment with a cat who didn't know I was in charge and a woman who didn't talk to me the right way, didn't reach down to scratch behind my ears, and probably wouldn't be feeding me any treats.

It was lonely. I had not been lonely before. In the shelter I had been with my mother and my sisters, and with other dogs who had shortly learned to follow my directions. Then I'd been with CJ. Now CJ was gone.

I sighed.

It was a very long morning.

At last I heard something from the hall—footsteps. There had been footsteps up and down it all morning, but none of them had been the right ones. Now I heard them, and a thrill seemed to vibrate through my whole body. I was at the door, quivering with impatience (and also with the need to pee) when CJ opened it.

"Shhh, Max. Easy, Max. I'm glad to see you, too," she said.

She dropped to her knees to pet me and rub both her hands down my body from my ears to my tail. I wiggled with pleasure. Finally she'd figured it out!

She was back to fix her mistake, and she wouldn't leave without me again.

But she didn't seem happy, and I couldn't understand why. I was here now! We were together! Why was her voice heavy? Why did her shoulders slump?

Jillian was still at the table, tapping that black plastic tray. I couldn't see why she wanted to do something so boring for so long, but it didn't matter. My girl was back!

"How was class?" Jillian asked, not looking up.

"Okay," CJ said, in a voice that meant nothing was okay.

"What did your teacher say about that thing you were drawing yesterday?"

CJ rolled her eyes. "He said it seemed *inauthentic*." Her voice was heavy on the last word.

"Does that mean he couldn't tell what it was, either?"

CJ dropped her backpack to the floor with a thud. I got ready to lift my leg against it.

"Max, no!" CJ cried out. She snatched up my leash from where it was hanging on the doorknob. "Max, wait!"

"I told you so!" Jillian said irritably, finally looking up from her tapping. "Dogs and apartments don't mix!"

CJ didn't answer, because we were hurrying outside. I had to wait until we were all the way on the sidewalk before she put me down and I could pee at last.

8

After I'd finished, CJ turned back to the apartment building, but then she turned around again. "Come on, Max," she muttered. "Let's get some fresh air. Well, sort of fresh. Well, it's air, anyway."

I was already tugging impatiently on the leash. I'd waited inside all morning! I was ready to be on the move at last, with CJ. I towed her down the walkway that led from the glass door of the apartment building to the sidewalk. Just where the two paths met, CJ hesitated.

The sidewalk was full of feet. Boots thumped, high heels clacked, sandals flopped, sneakers ran. A boy whizzed by on a skateboard. CJ jumped back. "Watch out, Max!" she said.

But I could smell something on that sidewalk that was too interesting to back away from. A stub of hot dog, less than an inch long, still nestled in a chunk of bun. Someone must have dropped it, and it was just lying there. Waiting. Waiting for me.

"Max!" CJ protested as I pulled with all my strength, tugging her onto the sidewalk and into the crowd going by.

I snatched up the hot dog and ate it in two gulps. Delicious! And then CJ and I were walking, with people all around us. Where were we going? I didn't know. It didn't matter. It was enough to be outside, in the city, in the warm sun, in the company of my girl.

CJ and I strolled along, and I could feel her grip on my leash ease up. I could tell that other dogs had been here before us. In one spot I smelled Duke, and in another Honey had peed on the sidewalk. I sniffed their marks extra hard.

As I sniffed, CJ slowed down to look into a store window. Then she speeded up to go around people sauntering more slowly than we were. I stayed right ahead of her, making sure everything was safe. Just like I was supposed to.

Up ahead I spotted a big square hole in the sidewalk, with a fence along one side. As we got closer, I could see that the hole had stairs going down inside it. Hot air full of smells wafted up. Interesting! I pulled CJ toward it.

She pulled back. I stopped. We stood at the top of the stairs. I wanted to go down there. It smelled like no place I'd ever been! Why were we waiting?

"Hey, are you going up or down?" an irritated voice said behind CJ.

She jumped to one side. "Uh. Sorry," she mumbled, mostly to me, as a tall teenage boy dressed all in black, from his spiky hair to his heavy boots, hurried down the steps, not pausing to glance at her.

CJ sighed, and her body seemed to sag a little. She tugged on the leash, pulling me away from the fascinating staircase. We went back to our walk.

"Look, it's CJ!" called out a voice.

I felt CJ tense up, and my muscles got tight, too. Maybe this was a threat. Maybe she needed my help.

Three girls came strolling along the sidewalk toward us. One had a backpack like CJ's, and the other two had slim cases they carried by their sides.

"Is that your dog?" the backpack girl said excitedly, when she got closer. "I love dogs! She's so cute!" She had boots on with long strings dangling from them. I was ready to grab one of those strings and give it a good pull when CJ bent down and picked me up.

"Uh, yeah," she mumbled. "This is Max. He's a boy. Careful, though. He's kind of nervous around strangers."

"Are you going to paint him, CJ?" asked one of the other girls. She had blond hair shaved nearly off on one side, long enough to fall over her shoulder on the other. I didn't like her voice much. It sounded sweet and kind, but there was something wrong with it—like a dog who puts his ears and tail down, trying to look meek, even though you can tell that he's still about to spring. This girl's voice was like that. It didn't mean what it pretended to mean.

"That would be *cute*," the other girl agreed. She stood with most of her weight on one foot, her hip out, her head tilted to one side. When dogs do that, they are trying to see something better. I don't know why humans do it, but I don't think that's the reason.

"Authentic," agreed the first girl, the blond one.

I could feel CJ cringe.

"That's a weird thing to say," said the girl with the boots, glancing at the other two as if they'd puzzled her.

"Well, no offense. I was only saying," said the blond girl.

The boots girl turned her attention to CJ. "Have you ever noticed that people always say 'no offense' like it's your fault they said something really offensive?" she asked. "Can I pet Max?"

She put a hand out without waiting for CJ to answer. I pulled my head up and showed her my teeth. It wasn't personal; she seemed nice enough. But she wasn't CJ.

The girl snatched her hand back.

"Wow, I guess CJ has a guard dog," said the blond girl. Her voice still sounded nice and not nice at once.

"Sorry," CJ mumbled. "I'm trying to teach him not to do that."

"Trying, not succeeding, huh?" the blond girl said. "Stella, are you coming or what?"

"Or what, I guess," Stella said.

Stella stood and looked at the other two for a few moments. I could tell they were trying to figure out who was in charge, just like I did with the other dogs at the park.

Stella won. The other two girls walked away. Stella glanced back at CJ and rolled her eyes.

"Like that's even an insult? That you have a guard

dog?" she said. "Pretty lame. How are you teaching Max not to bite?"

"Maybe you could help? If you don't mind?" CJ's voice was still quiet, but she looked hopeful. "Unless you've got somewhere to go. Or something. I don't mean to make you wait."

"No, I'm not going anywhere. Especially not with Laurel and Jenna. They're such snobs. How can I help with Max?"

Stella and CJ found a bench along the sidewalk and sat down. CJ put me on the bench between them and pulled the can of treats out of her pocket. My whole body sprang to attention. Treats!

"Now try to pet him again," she said. "Not on the top of his head; lots of dogs get a little scared if you do that first thing. Try under his chin or behind his ears. Okay, ready? Gentle, Max!"

Stella's hand came toward me. But she did it slowly, and CJ was right next to me, and most important, CJ had shaken a treat out of the can and into her hand. My attention was on that and not so much on Stella's hand.

Stella rubbed behind my ear. She wasn't as good at it as CJ was, but she wasn't bad. And CJ popped a treat into my mouth.

Delicious! Gentle, Max was starting to feel like a

good game. I crunched the treat and looked around for more.

"Hey, he didn't try to bite me!" Stella looked pleased. CJ was smiling.

"That's great! Would you do it again?"

Stella and CJ and I played Gentle, Max over and over again. I won every time and got a lot of treats. When CJ finally put the can back in her pocket (too bad!), she and Stella stayed on the bench, talking.

"You've really lived in New York all your life?" CJ asked.

"Yeah. Why not? You act surprised. Lots of people live here!" Stella said, laughing.

"I know. Too many!" CJ giggled a bit, too. "I just can't imagine living here all the time. How do you figure stuff out?"

"Like what?"

"Like . . . I don't know. Like how to cross the street!" Stella laughed harder. "No, really!" CJ insisted. "Nobody waits for a Walk signal, so you feel like a doofus standing there on the curb. But if I try to cross against the lights, people honk and yell. I just don't get it!"

Stella was still giggling. "I don't know. I just cross when everybody else does. The cars can't hit all of you. That's what my big brother always says, anyway. Do you like New York, though? Except for crossing the street?"

CJ shrugged, dropping her gaze and twisting her fingers in the fur along my back. "I haven't seen that much of it. Just the school where the art program is, and the apartment where I'm staying. And the dog park."

"The dog park? Why the dog park? I mean, I like dogs, too, but it's not the first place I'd go in New York."

CJ shrugged. "My mom said she'd send me an allowance so I'd have some spending money, but she didn't do it. She's . . . kind of like that. So I've been walking some dogs in the neighborhood on the weekends. Five bucks a dog. That's why I go to the dog park."

"Oh, I get it. But haven't you been sightseeing at all? That's too bad. Really. What about something simple, like Central Park? It's so much fun when the weather is nice and everybody's out biking and Rollerblading and playing Frisbee. And walking dogs, too! You should take Max!"

"I don't know . . ." CJ said. Her voice trailed off.

"You should," Stella said firmly. "Just look at him.

He's a New York dog—you can tell! He doesn't let anybody push him around. He'd love Central Park. You should definitely take him there."

"Maybe," CJ said softly. "Sometime."

CJ took me back home after saying good-bye to Stella, and spent the afternoon in her bedroom, rubbing her pencil on a big sheet of paper and frowning. I didn't understand why she was bothering to do that. Clearly it didn't make her happy, and after all, she had a dog to play with. Wasn't I better than a pencil?

I guess CJ figured out that I was, because she took me for a long walk and my own visit to the dog park before we settled in for another night.

In the morning I was surprised to find out that CJ had not learned her lesson, because she left me behind *again*! And this time Jillian put on her tall shoes, picked up a purse and that coat with the interesting collar, and left as well. Sneakers made it out into the hall this time, but Jillian grabbed her and shoved her back inside, then abruptly slammed the door shut.

I barked at the door a bit, but that didn't produce any interesting results. So I wandered around the apartment restlessly. When I felt a need to pee, I squatted near one of the kitchen cabinets and left a puddle on the floor.

Then I had to figure out what to do next.

Sneakers had stretched out on the carpet, lying in a patch of sunlight that came through the window. She had her back to me and seemed perfectly relaxed. Only her long gray tail, lying on the carpet, twitched from time to time.

It looked like the perfect moment to show Sneakers which pet was more important in this apartment. And that was going to be me.

9

I made sure everything about me told Sneakers that I was in charge and she was not. Head, ears, and tail lifted as high as I could get them. Legs stiff. Back straight. Hair along my spine bristling. My upper lip curled, ready to show my teeth.

Then I walked steadily toward the cat. This time she would understand.

Soon I was within a foot of her. She rolled over lazily and looked at me, her golden eyes glinting in the sunlight.

She didn't get up, and that was good. I could tell

she had gotten my message. She lay limp on her back, her belly showing. I'd finally convinced her!

Thrilled, I took another two steps forward. Somehow I knew exactly what to do. I'd stand over her, one paw on either side, to show her that there was no mistake. I was Max, and she was just Sneakers.

Then, without any warning, she changed the rules.

Suddenly, so quickly I hardly had time to react, she flipped over to her feet. Her lips pulled back, just like mine, to show a mouthful of teeth. That wasn't fair! She'd been lying on her back—that showed she was giving in. Now she was displaying her teeth—that showed she was ready to fight!

What did she *mean*? I was so confused that I paused for a second, and that second was long enough.

Sneakers's front paw lashed out and hit the side of my face. Claws pricked and stung. That hurt! I leaped back in astonishment and Sneakers shot over to the kitchen and leaped up onto the counter.

Unfair! Again! I was so enraged that I raced over to the kitchen, propped my feet up as high as they could go on a cabinet, and barked as loudly as I could.

Sneakers sat down, wrapped her tail snugly around

her back feet, and washed the paw that had swatted me.

I knew I was making a fool of myself, barking at a cat who didn't want to come down, but I couldn't help myself. Finally, Sneakers turned her back on me and began to wash her other paw, and I dropped back down to all fours in disgust.

I didn't know why it was so hard to convince Sneakers of what everybody else seemed to understand with no trouble—that I was the one in charge. But I was beginning to feel like it just wasn't worth trying to teach a cat manners.

I decided to show her that I didn't care what she did. I left the kitchen without looking back and headed for CJ's room.

It would be nice to curl up on the bed to wait for CJ to come back, but I couldn't jump that high. Frustrated, I stood on my back legs and stretched up with my front paws. No matter how tall I tried to make myself, I couldn't reach the top of the mattress. There was not a chance I could climb that high. If only CJ were here to lift me up!

Frustrated, I scrabbled with both paws at the bed. I didn't manage to get up on it, but something else happened. CJ's sky blue quilt began a slow-motion slide off the bed and ended up in a puffy pile on top of my head.

Buried in soft, warm cloth, I shook my head hard and barked with irritation. I was the boss! I was not supposed to be underneath a heap of material! I went in a circle but encountered nothing but more quilt. It wasn't very heavy, but I wasn't very big—it was getting hard to push my way through the soft folds.

There was quilt under my feet now, too. I trampled on it, forcing it down, and then put my head down and shoved.

I didn't get anywhere. It was as if the quilt was shoving back!

I bit it. That didn't help at all.

I pushed forward again, with no luck. Then I backed up a step so that I could push forward with more force.

My tail sprang free from the soft weight. I took another step backward and my rear legs were out in the open as well.

Backing up! That was the trick! I took step by careful step until at last my head and muzzle slipped out from under the quilt. Then I stepped on it to make sure it would stay on the ground where it belonged.

It was soft underfoot and smelled comfortingly of CJ. I turned in a circle, trampling myself a soft nest, and curled up with my nose and tail touching. I rested for a while, chewing on a corner of the quilt now and then, thinking of my girl. I even closed my eyes for a short nap.

When I woke up, I chewed the quilt some more, until fuzzy white feathers started drifting out. They stuck to my tongue and tasted very strange, so I stopped chewing, got up, and shook my head to get rid of them.

The feathery taste was still on my tongue, so I headed into the kitchen for a drink of water. Sneakers was still on the counter. She had stretched out for another nap. I never knew an animal who could sleep so much.

I ignored her. Without even a glance at the cat, I began to sniff around the kitchen floor, smelling CJ's footprints and Jillian's, finding some crumbs left over from CJ's breakfast toast. I stepped around the puddle I'd left on the floor earlier—it's not terribly interesting to smell your own urine—and sniffed until I got to a cupboard with the most entrancing aroma.

Food. It smelled like food.

I sniffed hard at the crack between the door and

the cabinet. Then I nudged with my nose, trying to get the door open.

No luck.

I scratched with my paw, then with both paws, scrabbling at the painted wood. Sneakers's head appeared over the edge of the counter, peering down at me. I paid her no attention. I had something more important to do.

The door didn't open. I was on one side and the food was on the other—this was not right. Something had to be done.

I stopped scratching and stared at the cupboard door. Then I put a paw against the wood and pushed.

The door didn't open. But I noticed something.

When I pushed, the door didn't go anywhere. But when I took my paw off, the door sprang open just a crack.

It wasn't open, not exactly. But it wasn't completely closed, either.

I tried to force my nose into the crack, but that only shoved the door all the way shut.

I was so frustrated I sat back on my haunches and growled at the door. That didn't do any good, either.

I pushed a paw against it once more.

Sneakers jumped down from the counter to land with a thump on the kitchen floor beside me. I ignored her and nosed at the door again, once more closing it completely.

Sneakers sniffed at the door, too.

I pushed at the door as hard as I could with my paw. The crack appeared again, but it was not any wider.

Before I could try to work my nose into the crack, however, Sneakers reached out her own paw. It was slimmer than mine, and she shot out those claws that had pricked my face so painfully before. It's so odd how cats keep their claws inside their feet like that!

As I stared, astonished, she batted at the cupboard door with her paw and made the crack wider. Wide enough for my nose!

I shouldered the cat aside and pushed with my whole head. The cupboard door swung open wide, and there inside was the paper bag that smelled so delicious.

Sneakers seemed to think it smelled good, too. She pushed her head into the cupboard right beside mine. I chewed at a corner of the bag. She sniffed hard, then reached in and ripped at the colorful paper. Her claws made a rent. That meant I could get my teeth into a scrap of paper and yank, twisting my head, even growling a little.

A chunk of paper tore loose, and I staggered backward. And food came out! Little brown pellets of food rushed out of the bag and cascaded all over the kitchen floor.

Delicious! Marvelous!

I had my head down and was gobbling up as much food as I could. Sneakers did the same. Maybe I should have chased her away, but there was so much food—plenty for both of us, really. Besides, those claws of hers were quite sharp.

We ate together. At last I was so full I couldn't stuff in another bite. It was a shame to leave so much food all over the floor of the kitchen, but my stomach was starting to hurt. Maybe we could come back and finish up later.

I slurped a little water from my bowl and headed back to CJ's room to sleep off that huge meal, curling up on her quilt once more.

To my surprise, Sneakers came with me. I was too full and sleepy to argue when she found a spot for herself on the quilt and began to make a strange rumbling noise that seemed to come from deep inside her throat. It sounded like a growl, and yet it was full of contentment and satisfaction.

Cats are very strange, I decided. There is no telling what they mean. And they are frustrating, the way they refuse to understand obvious things, like the fact that they are supposed to do what I want them to.

But it felt comforting to have her nearby, even so. It reminded me of sleeping huddled in a heap with my sisters and my mother, back in my days at the shelter. And it would have been more difficult to get that cupboard door open without her, so maybe . . . just maybe . . . it would be all right to have her around.

I yawned.

Of course I was still the most important animal in the apartment. But Sneakers wasn't so bad.

I closed my eyes and settled down for my second nap of the morning. I was so deeply asleep that I didn't hear the door open and close. I didn't hear high-heeled shoes clacking across the floor.

I did hear Jillian's voice, however, raised in a loud screech. It jolted me into wakefulness. Sneakers jerked up her head as well.

The door opened and closed again, and a familiar scent reached my nose. CJ! At last! And I hadn't been at the door to greet her!

I staggered up—my stomach still hurt a little—and hurried into the living room as quickly as I could. CJ was standing by the closet, and Jillian was in the doorway to the kitchen, talking angrily, waving her hands in the air.

"I'm sorry. I'm sorry," CJ was saying meekly. "I'll clean it up. I'm sorry."

CJ needed me to protect her! I leaped to her side. It wasn't much of a leap, honestly. I was so full from that meal and still a bit sleepy.

But I got to CJ's side and turned around to show Jillian my teeth.

"No, Max! Gentle, Max!" CJ dropped to her knees and grabbed me.

"And now it's growling at me!" Jillian said, her voice rising to a higher screech. "That's it. That's the last straw. I told you dogs don't belong in this city, but you talked me into giving it a chance. Well, it's not working out. It's just not."

CJ gasped. She squeezed me to her, a little too tightly, but I didn't complain. I could tell she needed me.

"Oh, don't look at me like that!" Jillian said, and then she let out a huge, loud sigh. "Look, CJ. I'm sorry, I am, but you've got to see that this is impossible. You're not here to take care of that thing, and it barks all day, and it pees on the floor, and—"

"He's just a puppy!" CJ said, her voice trembling. "All puppies bark. They all pee. They can't help it!"

"We had a deal," Jillian said more sternly. "And now I come home to a mess in the kitchen, and I can see that dog isn't safe to be around. There's no way I'm letting it stay here!"

"I can't take him back to the shelter. I can't!" CJ begged. "They'll put him to sleep!"

Jillian stood up straighter. "Then you'll have to find him another home."

CJ got up, holding me, and hustled me into her room, where she shut the door on me. How unfair! How ridiculous! I began to bark to remind her that we should always be together. Sneakers shook her head, rattling her collar, and jumped off the bed.

I heard Jillian's voice doing more of the angry talking and CJ's voice doing more of the "I'm sorrys." I heard a broom rustling across the kitchen floor and food pellets clinking into the trash.

Then CJ pushed open her door. Sneakers seized the chance to shoot across the room and escape, but I ran to CJ, barking impatiently.

She was very sad. I had to get to work right away. She sat down on the floor and groaned when she saw the quilt. I scrambled onto her lap and stood up on my hind legs to nuzzle my nose into her neck.

"Oh, Max," she whispered. "Oh, Max. I'm so sorry, Max."

Her cheeks were wet and salty. I licked at them.

"She won't let me keep you. I begged and begged,

but she won't. And she says I've only got a week to find you another home. Listen, Max, you have to be nice. You have to be good, or nobody's going to want you. And if nobody wants you, you'll go back to the shelter, and then . . . Oh, please, *please,* be good, Max. Please."

I was glad to hear that I was good. I was glad I could lick CJ's tears away. I would always be there to do that. I'd take care of her whenever she was sad, or scared, or lonely. I'd be her dog forever.

But I hoped we'd go outside for a walk soon. After such a big meal, I needed to.

10

The next morning Jillian and CJ both left *again*. I immediately went to the kitchen and pawed at the food cupboard, but this time there was a new plastic contraption on the handle and the door didn't open no matter what I did.

Sneakers didn't come to help, either. She had settled in along the back of the couch for a snooze, so I couldn't even curl up next to her and feel her warmth.

Restlessly, I wandered around the apartment. There was a closet near the front door, where Jillian kept her shoes and a few umbrellas. She'd opened it that morning long enough to grab her purse, and it hadn't shut all the way before she left.

I nosed it open. There was stuff inside that I hadn't smelled before, and this seemed as good a time as any.

I investigated Jillian's boots and shoes thoroughly. Then I looked up.

Jillian's coat was hanging from a hook. I stood on my back legs to smell it properly. It smelled like the street—of car exhaust and dirt and grime and food and people, lots and lots of people, all in a hurry, all with somewhere to go. I loved that smell. I wished I were out in the street right now, with CJ, instead of stuck in here with a cat who just wanted to sleep the day away.

I took the hem of the coat in my mouth. I gave it an experimental tug.

It must not have been on the hook very securely, because it came down on my head with a flop that startled me. I remembered how to get out from under something like that, however, and backed away until I was free.

The coat had a wonderful collar made of soft gray fur. It smelled interesting—better than interesting. Fascinating. It was an animal type of smell, an animal that I hadn't ever met. But something deep inside me recognized it. It was something that I needed to chase and catch.

I gripped the fur as tightly as I could with my teeth. I shook my head a little, wrestling with it. It felt good. I braced my feet and began to drag the coat with me across the floor.

The door banged open.

"Max, no!" CJ wailed. I dropped the coat and ran to her, wagging. She was back! She'd hardly been gone any time at all, and now she was back!

Sneakers perked up and leaped off the couch, making a beeline for the door, but CJ kicked it shut before the cat could get there and dropped to her knees to snatch the coat away from me.

I thought that was unfair. I wasn't done playing with it! Still, I didn't intend to complain, not now that my girl was here. She stuffed the coat back in the closet, shut the door securely, grabbed both me and my leash, and hustled me out the door, pushing Sneakers back inside with her foot as we made it out into the hallway.

That should let Sneakers know who was the more important pet, I thought in triumph. I got to go outside for walks with my girl, and Sneakers had to stay shut up inside, or at most make it out into the hallway. Obviously, dogs were much, much better than cats. I hoped she'd finally get the message.

As soon as we were outside, CJ set me down.

"Come on, Max, hurry up," she muttered. "It's just a fifteen-minute break. I've got to get back to class!"

I was about to pee on a scraggly little bush when I caught a whiff of a familiar scent. It was a dog—a dog I'd met before. It was Baxter.

I looked up and saw the big male and his owner walking down the sidewalk. In less than a minute, they'd turn onto the little walkway that led to the door of Jillian's apartment building.

Last time I'd met Baxter, CJ had picked me up before I'd managed to teach him to respect me. This was my chance! I sprang toward the street, barking loudly. CJ hadn't been holding my leash very tightly, and I yanked it right out of her hand.

Baxter saw me and heard me and smelled me, too. He lunged forward against his own leash. He didn't bark; maybe he couldn't, since his collar was so tight now he was breathing with little choking noises. But a low growl was starting deep in his chest, rising in his throat, spilling out between his teeth.

"Max! No!" CJ shrieked.

Baxter's owner laughed as CJ raced after me and snatched me up. No fair! How was I supposed to teach Baxter the rules when I was up here and he was down there?

I squirmed in CJ's grip, but she didn't let go. She backed away into a bush, holding me tight, as Baxter and his owner turned onto the walkway. Baxter was still straining against the leash, trying to get to us, and I was wrestling with CJ's hands, trying to get down to him.

"That runt needs to learn some street smarts!" Baxter's owner said. He seemed to think something was funny.

"Could you take Baxter in, please," CJ said tightly. "I don't want to put Max down while he's here."

"At least one of you has some sense!" the man said, and he dragged Baxter, still growling, down the walk and inside the building.

Once the doors slid shut behind the two of them, CJ put me down. I ran up to the glass door and barked ferociously at Baxter, but he didn't even turn his head to look at me. What nerve!

I went back to the bush and finished what I'd been doing. Then I looked up happily at CJ and wagged, ready to go places with my girl.

But the next thing CJ did was very strange. She scooped me up and rushed me back inside the build-

116

ing! She didn't even wait for the elevator, but ran up the stairs, holding me against her chest. It was a bumpy, jolting ride.

Then she unlocked the door and dumped me inside next to Sneakers, shutting the door so quickly neither of us had time to get out.

I sat back on my haunches and barked with dismay. Sneakers walked disdainfully away and lay down under Jillian's desk. What had happened to my walk with CJ? Why had she rushed off like that?

I barked once more and then left the door alone, feeling as if I needed to growl, except I wasn't sure what to growl *at*. It wasn't right that my girl kept leaving me. I'd been through a lot to find her, and now that I had, we were supposed to stay together. Why didn't CJ realize this? Why did she keep going away?

I forgave her, though, when she came back later and didn't seem in such a rush. She petted me and Sneakers both. Then she took my leash and her backpack, and we went outside for a walk—a *real* walk, this time.

I pulled CJ along the sidewalk, my nose down, enjoying all the smells. My ears twitched to the whoosh of cars rushing past, the blasts of music from the windows, the words from the people we passed on the street—sometimes angry, sometimes happy, sometimes calm, always loud enough to be heard over the noise all around us.

It was marvelous, after a morning in the quiet apartment, to be out here with the sounds and the smells and all the feet on every side. When we got to the hole in the sidewalk with stairs going down, CJ hesitated once more at the top.

I did not want to hesitate, however. Warm air gusted up, full of smells I had never met before—metal, oil, something warm and mechanical that almost seemed alive in a strange new way. I started down the steps eagerly, towing CJ after me.

At the bottom of the stairs, CJ stood and fiddled with a machine against a wall for a while, and then picked me up and carried me through a strange sort of gate. Once we were on the other side, she stopped and looked around. There were several staircases here, and hallways that led off in different directions, and people hurrying past.

"Cute dog!" someone said.

A woman in a long, rippling dress stopped to smile at us, reaching out to me. "Gentle, Max!" CJ said firmly.

"Gentle, Max!" usually meant a treat. I looked

around alertly for something tasty to eat. It didn't come, but as I was waiting for it, the lady in the dress gave my ears a quick scratch.

"Such a sweetie," the woman said, smiling.

I looked up impatiently at CJ. Where was my treat?

"Thanks," CJ said. She still didn't remember to reward me for winning the game. I was starting to learn that people do not always remember to play games properly. They're still better than cats, though.

"Um, do you know which train I take to get to Central Park?" CJ asked the woman.

"Try the C line. Downtown," the woman said. When CJ still looked confused, she pointed. "Use that staircase. But the rule is no dogs unless they're in a bag."

"Oh." CJ sounded dismayed. "I didn't know that. Maybe we shouldn't have . . ."

"I wouldn't worry about it," the woman said cheerfully. "You've got a backpack; use that. People get quite creative—look over there!" She pointed, and CJ's head turned. I looked where my girl was looking.

A man was walking up one of the staircases, and he had a backpack on his back. A beagle with soft, floppy ears was inside the backpack! Its back legs were in the pack, and its front legs and head rested on the man's shoulder. They both seemed content. The man walked quickly by us without stopping, and CJ's eyes widened in amazement.

I stared, too. It seemed like an odd way for a dog to be with his human. I'd rather be walking, pulling CJ along on the leash, leading us wherever we should go. How would that beagle protect his person if they ran into something dangerous?

But CJ must have thought it was a good idea, because after the woman in the dress waved good-bye, my girl sat down on a bench and put me beside her. Then she took off her backpack, rearranged her papers and pencils and markers so that they all fit in a single section, picked me up, and tucked me inside another.

This part of the backpack was big enough to hold my whole body, and I wasn't any too pleased about being in there. It was dark and it shut me in from all the interesting smells around me. I shook my head and barked and scrabbled with my paws.

"Easy, Max, wait a second!" CJ said. I heard the buzzing sound of a zipper, and then there was a space for me to poke my head out. That was better. I could see and smell what was happening and keep an eye on CJ.

"Just be good," CJ told me. "Good Max." She fed

me a few treats and petted me until I finally got the idea that she wanted me to stay in this strange place. It was odd, but I supposed I could do it, for a little while. Since it was CJ who was asking.

She didn't put the backpack on her back, like the beagle's owner had done. I was glad about that. She held me in her arms and carried me down the stairs. There was a cement platform at the bottom, with some other people waiting. We joined them.

Lower than the platform where we were standing, two metal tracks ran a long distance, disappearing into a tunnel to the right and another one to the left. I kept my head out of the backpack, peering around with interest, and then I perked up my ears and strained my nose, sniffing as hard as I could.

Something was coming.

I felt puffs of hot air swirling around me, ruffling my fur. The air smelled even more strongly of what I had first noticed when I had been standing on the sidewalk—something metallic and oily, but different from the cars that whizzed back and forth on the streets. Something dark and mysterious and exciting.

Now it was arriving.

It came out of a dark tunnel with a roar and a flash of bright light. I squirmed to get out of the backpack, trying to get a good look at the thing as it rocketed past us, but CJ held me tightly. I even barked at it, wanting it to slow down so I could see it better.

A few people nearby chuckled.

Then the thing *did* slow down to a creaky stop in front of us. Doors slid open, just like the elevator doors. Inside there were lights and people. Lots of people. Some were sitting on brightly colored seats; some were standing and holding on to shiny metal poles. Together the people and the train made up the smell that had so puzzled me. Metal and oil and heat and human beings, all together.

"Okay, here's the train," CJ muttered. She took a deep breath and carried me inside.

We found a seat next to a window, and CJ set both me and the backpack on her lap. With my rear legs and rump inside the pack, I put my front paws up against the glass as we began to move. This thing called a train, I realized, was something like the car I had ridden in to get to the park where I'd first met CJ. It was moving, like that car, and it would take me somewhere new.

Meanwhile, I wished I could get my nose out of the window to sniff up the rushing air outside. I could tell it smelled wonderful, of dirt and damp and garbage and small scuttling animals. CJ made a funny little sound when she saw one of those scamper across the tracks, dragging a strange, hairless tail. But I wished I could get out and chase it. It would be even better than the collar of Jillian's coat.

The train raced along, rocking us both gently. It stopped and started again and again. After one of the stops, a woman, older than CJ, got on the train and sat down on the seat next to us. She had long brown hair that spilled down around her shoulders and dangling earrings that made fascinating tinkling noises, but I was much more interested in what she had on her lap.

It was a soft cloth carrier, sort of a cube, with a handle on top and mesh panels on all four sides. And peeking out of one panel was a dog!

It was a small dog (although, I had to admit it, still a bit bigger than me) with floppy white fur that fell over its face. I squirmed around in the backpack so that I could get my nose closer. The new dog was a female, and she smelled scared. She didn't like her carrier, I could tell. She didn't like the rocking and rattling of the train. So she wasn't in any mood to challenge me or try to tell me what to do.

I touched my nose to the mesh panel, but the dog

inside was so unhappy, she was not even interested in sniffing me back. She just curled up with her muzzle down on her paws, ignoring me. How dull. Looking out the window was more fun, so I turned back to that.

When the train stopped again, the woman got up without a word and took her carrier and her dog with her.

"You were a good boy, Max," CJ said softly to me. "I guess that's how New Yorkers do it, huh? If you don't bother people on the subway, they don't bother you."

The next time the train stopped, CJ got up and carried me out. We went up some more stairs and out onto the sidewalk, where Stella was standing, waving wildly at CJ.

She wasn't wearing boots today; instead, she had on silver sandals with black stars on them. "See, you did it!" she said happily when CJ and I got to her side. "You rode the subway! Totally like a real New Yorker. And I'm so glad you brought Max! Look, I got some treats for him. Let's see if he remembers me. Gentle, Max!"

Stella remembered how to play Gentle, Max better than CJ did. I got *two* treats from her, plus a reasonably good ear scratch.

Then CJ set me down and I noticed something. There was a stone wall next to the sidewalk, and a gate in the wall. On the other side of that gate I could smell warm dirt and grass and growing things. I could also smell that other dogs had been through the gate. *Lots* of other dogs.

I pulled CJ toward it. "Look, Max knows where we're going!" Stella said. "I told you he'd like Central Park! And it's your first real New York landmark, right, CJ? Come on, let's go!"

Many of the dogs had left their marks on the gate or the wall. I added my own, on top, as it should be, to tell them all who had been here. Me, Max. Then I led us all through into a park, sort of like the one where I had first met CJ. But bigger. Much, much bigger.

Paths branched and curved over lawns of smooth grass. There were trees and bushes and garbage cans that I could smell from where we stood. And there were people—walking and running along the paths, riding bikes, pushing strollers. Some stretched out on the grass or sat on benches, reading books or holding papers or tapping on their phones.

I set off into the park, pulling CJ along behind me. She and Stella kept talking as I sniffed and sniffed. So many dogs had been along this path—too many to keep track of! Some marks were fresh; others were fading. Those dogs were about to meet me, and I had to show them who I was. That I was Max.

11

"I don't know," I heard CJ say to Stella as I towed her over to a garbage can. "Everybody else is so much better than I am. It was one thing to be good at art back home, but here . . ."

A half-full cup of ice cream had landed on the pavement beside the can, oozing chocolate goop into a nearby wrapper smeared with grease and ketchup. Wonderful!

"Don't be dumb," Stella said.

"Oh, thanks, that's nice," CJ answered.

"No, really. They don't let you into this program if you don't have talent! How many times did you apply?"

"Just this time."

"Seriously? I tried for three years to get in before I made it. See what I mean?"

"Well, maybe— Max! Stop that!" CJ pulled at my leash to drag me away before I'd finished. Oh, well. There were many other interesting smells to investigate.

I led the girls farther into the park, my nose busy with every step. Sometimes their words drifted to my ears between sniffs.

When I heard my name, my ears perked up.

"She said you can't keep Max? CJ, that's so unfair! It's horrible!"

"I know it is! I know it's horrible!" CJ said, and her voice wavered. "She just . . . she doesn't like dogs at all. She doesn't get it, how puppies act. And what am I supposed to do about it? It's not like I can just leave and take Max with me!"

I hesitated. It sounded like my girl needed me to take care of her . . . but there was something interesting up ahead. A smell was wafting toward me on a warm breeze that pulled all my attention forward.

I'd take care of CJ later. After all, I'd always be her dog. Right now, I had to sniff.

"So I've got to find him a new home. I've *got* to.

Before next Tuesday!" CJ went on. "Or he has to go back to the shelter."

"Poor Max!"

Poor Max didn't seem to be the same thing as Gentle, Max. It did not involve treats. So I focused on the smell up ahead. My entire body tensed. My ears tipped forward. My tail went up.

Dogs. I could smell dogs.

I charged ahead, pulling CJ behind me. We cut through a little stand of trees and into a meadow where dogs were running everywhere.

Some of them were chasing Frisbees or balls that their owners had thrown. Some were just racing in big circles, barking with delight. A few were snoozing under trees. This was much bigger than the dog park near Jillian's apartment, and there were many more dogs. All of them were about to find out that I was Max!

I quivered and barked until CJ took off my leash, and then I charged straight ahead.

I heard Stella gasp. "Oh, Max, no!" she cried out. "That's a rottweiler!"

"It's okay," I heard CJ reassure her. "Max can handle anything."

Then I stopped listening to them, because all my attention was focused on the dog heading for me.

He was huge. His jowly head was the size of my entire body! His muzzle and feet were brown; his body was black and seemed made entirely of muscle.

He bounded forward, excitement in his eyes, his ears flapping in the wind. I raced to meet him. Just before he got to me, he bowed down on the grass, front legs low, back legs high, stump of a tail wiggling energetically. Everything about him said, "Let's play!"

I paused and stood as tall as I could. This brought me to eye level with him, since his chin was on the grass.

He stayed down in his bow, his tail wagging harder than ever. He knew I was in charge. He knew that I was Max. That was good.

Now we could have fun.

I bowed back, and he dashed away, so I chased him. He didn't run too fast, though, and he kept looking back at me, which slowed him down. That meant I could stay close at his heels. We made a big loop over the grass and doubled back toward CJ and Stella.

Then the rottweiler flopped down on his back on the grass. I knew what to do! I charged for his face, biting at his muzzle. They were pretend bites; I didn't

intend to hurt him. We were just playing. Even so, I still planned to win.

He swatted me aside with an enormous paw, and I went tumbling in the grass. I heard CJ cry out, "Oh!" but I didn't stop. I just rolled upright and charged back at my friend and opponent.

He was still lying down, so I seized one ear and tugged at it. He rolled. I flopped down on top of his head and tried to wrestle him down. He got up and shook his head, sending me onto my nose on the ground.

I heard CJ and Stella laughing, but I didn't stop. "Boy, that's one fierce little guy!" said a new voice.

A young man was standing over us with a leash. "Come on, Tigger," he said, clipping the leash onto the rottweiler's collar. "Time to go."

I stood and barked after my new friend as his owner led him away. I wasn't done playing! But he didn't come back, and I was a little tired, so I came over to CJ and lay beside her for a rest.

Stella and CJ and I played Gentle, Max for a while with Stella's treats, and as we did, the girls talked.

"It's so unfair that your mom's friend won't let you keep him. He's completely adorable!" Stella said, stroking my back after she'd given me a treat. I allowed it. I was busy chewing anyway.

"He's not adorable with everybody," CJ said with a sigh. "But he's learning. He really is! I wish you could take him."

"I wish I could, too," Stella said sadly, taking her hand away. "My little sister's allergic to *everything*. Mom says we can get a goldfish, but who wants a goldfish? I want a pet I can *pet*. CJ, there's got to be something you can do. It's too bad you and Max can't run away together. Do you know that book about the two kids who run away to the Met? The big art museum? That would be cool, living in an art museum."

"I think . . ." CJ stopped petting me and hesitated for a moment. "Running away isn't as easy as it sounds in books," she said at last. "Or I'd do it. I'd take Max and run back home, anyway."

"CJ, you can't just leave art school right in the middle!" Stella said.

CJ shrugged. "It doesn't matter. I can't drive, and I don't have money for the bus, and I'm not about to hitchhike. Anyway, my mom's not there. She took off for the summer. So the house is all shut up."

"Okay, I wasn't serious about running away," Stella told her. "Even to the Met. So let's think. Max can't stay with you, and he can't stay with me, and you can't take him home."

"There are millions of people in this city," CJ said glumly, taking a turn with the scratching. "And none of them want Max."

"Come on, that's way too gloomy, CJ. It's not like you've asked every single person in New York! I'll help. What have you tried?"

"I put up a notice in the lobby of Jillian's apartment building," CJ said. "And one at school. With my phone number. But nobody's called yet."

"I saw that one on the school bulletin board. But CJ, it doesn't even have a picture of Max! And you only put up two? That's not enough. We have to get the word out way wider than that."

"I asked all my dog-walking clients. But they have dogs already. I mean, obviously. What else am I supposed to do? Back home I'd talk to all my friends, and the teachers at school, and everybody I know. But here—I don't even know anybody else to ask!"

"Everybody," Stella said firmly. "We'll ask *everybody*. Posters, for a start. With a photo of Max!" She took out her phone from her pocket, but then she put it back. "No, there's a better way. CJ, you've got to draw a picture of him."

"Me?" CJ sounded startled. I perked up my ears and looked around alertly, in case there was a threat to my girl nearby.

But nothing seemed alarming, so I lowered my head and leaned it into CJ's fingers for more scratching.

"Of course! I saw that painting you did a few days ago. Of the brown dog? That's your dog back home, right?"

"Yeah. Molly. Jenna said it was 'cute,'" CJ said with a sigh.

"Oh, forget Jenna. It was completely adorable! Way better than a photo. Go on, do a drawing of Max right now. And we'll get it made up into a poster and put them all over the neighborhood. It'll work. I know it will."

To my dismay, CJ stopped scratching in order to get a pad of paper and a packet of long, thin sticks out of her bag. She looked carefully at me and began to make scratching motions on the paper with the tip of one of the sticks.

Why would anybody want to scratch paper instead of a dog? Since CJ had transferred her attention from me to this strange activity with the sticks, I was ready to do more running and to find another friend to wrestle with. But Stella fed me more treats so I stayed put for a little while.

"That's it; that's perfect!" Stella exclaimed happily,

peering at CJ's paper. "You got his eyes just right. Anybody would want to adopt that little thing! Okay, give it to me. I'll make a bunch of posters. We'll put them up everywhere. We'll find Max a home!"

She petted me and jumped up, said good-bye to CJ, and dashed off in her silver sandals.

CJ stayed on the grass, looking out over the lawn where the dogs were running and wrestling, fetching balls, sleeping, scratching, being petted, and running back to do it all over again.

"See, Jillian's wrong. People do have dogs in New York," she murmured, ruffling the fur along my spine until I let out a little groan of happiness. "Oh, Max."

I looked up at her alertly and cocked my head, hearing the sadness in her voice. Then I turned and nudged her hand, which had paused in its scratching. I knew it made her happy to pet me. It made me happy, too. It was silly how often I had to remind her of that fact.

"My dog back home, Molly . . ." CJ said to me, and her voice trailed off. She sighed. "I needed Molly so much, Max. I was younger when I got her, and stuff at home . . . it wasn't so great. But you—it's different with you. You need *me*. I just wish Jillian could see that!"

The scratching didn't seem to be doing its job of making CJ happy, because she picked me up all of a sudden and buried her face in my fur. I licked her cheeks and wagged, and she sighed and lowered me to her lap.

I licked at her fingers. But I was getting restless. There were more dogs out there, and I hadn't taught them all to respect me yet.

"Okay, go on, go play," CJ said, just a little shakily.

I licked her hand one last time, and then a dog caught my eye, a Great Dane who reminded me of Duke. I charged off to see what kind of game he might be interested in.

He had a rope toy in his mouth. I grabbed one end and pulled as hard as I could, growling fiercely. He shook his head so that I flopped over onto my side in the grass, but I never let go of the rope. He towed me all over the lawn.

After my game of pull-the-rope with my Great Dane friend, I went on to play tag with a shih tzu who was about my size. Then I got right into the middle of a game of it's-my-stick-no-it's-mine with a golden retriever whose long fur rippled as she ran and a brown mutt with one white eye. In between playing I ran back to CJ, who petted and praised me and told me I was a good boy.

Of course I am. I'm Max.

Each time I checked on CJ, she was scratching on the paper with her sticks. She'd glance up at the scene in front of her, her eyes bright with interest, and then look back at her paper, making quick strokes with her pencil, sometimes smudging them with her thumb. She'd show me when I came panting up.

"Look, Max," she'd say. "That's you with that golden." For some reason she held a piece of paper in front of my face. "Silly dog, you hardly let her have a turn with that stick. And look at this—it's the boy over there throwing a Frisbee for his Lab. Doesn't that look like fun? But you're not going to be able to catch a Frisbee, Max, no, you're not."

"Hey, that's really cool," said a voice behind us.

I looked up and there was a boy a few years older than CJ, with a black Lab sitting and panting by his side.

"Are you doing sketches of the dogs? Can I buy one of Alice?" he asked, rubbing his dog's ears.

I pranced up to Alice, ready to do more wrestling or chasing, but she merely lay down and looked at me. I put a paw on her head. She sighed and didn't move.

"Oh," CJ said. Her face turned warm and pink. "I wasn't—I was just—I mean, I'm not selling them."

The boy looked disappointed. I was disappointed, too. This black Lab was not any fun at all.

"But you can have it," CJ said quickly. "If you really want it. Do you?" She ripped a page out of the sketchbook and offered it to the boy. He brightened up.

"Really? I can have it? Thanks, that's amazing!" I heard him say as I wandered off to find another dog who was ready to have more fun.

Not long after that, CJ clipped my leash back on my collar. On our way out of the park, she stopped at a cart that smelled so wonderful I started to drool and bought a hot dog in a bun and a bottle of water. She sat on a bench and lifted me up to share the delicious, salty meat. I did not care for the bun smeared with yellow and green stuff that smelled sharp enough to make my eyes water, so she ate that herself. Then she poured some of the water in her hand for me to lap up.

"I didn't know there was a place like this in the city, Max," she said after she swallowed. "People are . . . kind of relaxed here. They're not in such a hurry. It's . . . you know what? It's fun. Or it would be if I wasn't worried about you."

I was full from the hot dog and tired out after all of my hard work at the dog park, so I crawled into CJ's lap and fell asleep. I didn't wake up even when she tucked me into her backpack for a return trip on the subway. When I opened my eyes at last, we were riding up in the elevator to Jillian's apartment. It felt good to be home with my girl.

12

I began to get used to the idea that CJ would go away from me in the mornings. I didn't like it, but there seemed to be nothing I could do to stop her.

Sometimes Jillian went away, too, and sometimes she stayed in the apartment and stared at her plastic box and made tapping noises on the flat tray. It didn't matter much whether she was there or not, though, since she never paid any attention to me.

I wasn't much interested in her, either. I did wish I could have some more fun with that coat of hers, the one that had such a fascinating collar. But the closet door always stayed shut and I couldn't get it to open, no matter how much I pawed at it. Sneakers never came to help.

Most of the time Sneakers and I ignored each other. But occasionally, when both CJ and Jillian were gone and I was very bored, I'd find her where she was sleeping and curl up next to her, so that I could feel the warmth of her soft gray body alongside mine.

Now and then she would make that rumbly sound deep inside. I had learned that it wasn't a growl, although I still had no idea what it meant. But I could feel it vibrating against my skin, and it was soothing.

Two days after CJ and I had gone to the big park, I woke up from a nap with Sneakers to discover that CJ had come home without my noticing! She was sitting cross-legged on the floor beside us, her sketch pad in her hand, scratching the paper furiously with her stick.

I jumped up, barking with excitement, and hurtled into her lap. Sneakers got to her feet, too, shook herself so that her collar jangled, gave me a disdainful look, and walked away to sit with her back to us and her tail wrapped tightly around her feet. She peeked back over her shoulder to see if we had noticed that she was annoyed with us.

"Oh, Max, I was almost finished!" CJ said. She hugged me close to her face as I happily licked her cheeks. "I wanted another picture of you. To keep. For later . . ." She sighed and put me down into her lap. I loved it when she put one hand on either side of my head and then ran them both down my body all the way to my rump. "You're not much of a model, you know? If Stella's not around to feed you treats, I have to catch you sleeping! Come on, let's go out for a walk."

She got my leash and I gave Sneakers a triumphant look. She didn't learn her lesson, though, since she tried to sneak out with us. CJ had to sweep the door shut right in her face. "Sorry, Sneakers!" she called, and we went out into the neighborhood.

Stella was waiting for us outside, wearing glittery pink flip-flops, and she and CJ walked up and down block after block. I sniffed out which other dogs had been there before me and how long ago they'd passed by. I recognized Honey on a bush and Baxter on a fire hydrant and Duke so high up on a wall that I couldn't cover his mark with my own no matter how hard I tried. How annoying!

While I was busy, Stella and CJ used tape and staples to put pieces of paper up on every surface they could—walls, poles, doors.

Some people stopped to look at the papers. Lots

of them said my name. "Max?" they asked. "Max needs a home?"

A few of them played Gentle, Max with me. It was amazing how many people knew that game. Some of them took a paper or two with them.

"I'll ask around," they'd say.

Or, "I'll put one up at my office."

Or, "Good luck. Hope you find something for him."

I got a little impatient since we had to stop so often to put up papers and talk to people. I wanted to keep walking, to explore more and more of the city, to find new things to smell and maybe new dogs to boss around.

CJ seemed pleased, though. "People are so nice," she said to Stella. "I didn't think they'd be so nice."

"It's going to work," Stella said firmly. "I know it will!"

CJ sighed. "I hope you're right."

Then the three of us went back home and played chase-the-paper-balls with Sneakers in the hallway.

The next morning, CJ took me out to pee as she usually did. But after we went back to the apartment, she did something odd. She crawled back into bed and pulled the covers up.

I was surprised. She was normally running around putting her sketchbook and pencils into her backpack and gobbling down breakfast at this time of the day. Had she forgotten what she was supposed to do?

It looked like it was my job to remind her. I put my paws up as high as I could reach on the bed and barked at her.

"Max, shush!" she mumbled, putting a hand down to pet me. "It's Saturday. I want to sleep late."

She didn't understand. I barked some more.

"Max, quiet!" She rolled over, reached both hands down over the edge of the bed, and picked me up. "You'll wake up Jillian."

"Too late," said a voice from the doorway to CJ's room. Jillian, wearing a bathrobe, gave me an irritated look. "How is it going with . . ." She hesitated a little. "You know. Finding somewhere for it to go. I saw all your posters."

CJ sat up in bed. "I don't know yet," she answered, not looking at Jillian.

"Oh. Well." Jillian turned and walked into the kitchen. I smelled the dark, bitter scent of the drink people called coffee.

"Oh, Max." CJ sighed, and she flopped back down on her pillow. I burrowed my nose into her neck and licked her enthusiastically. I still didn't understand why she wasn't getting up, but if she wanted to lie in bed and play with me, that was all right, too. I tugged at a strand of her hair, and when she pushed me away, I wrestled with her hand until she groaned and giggled at the same time.

"Okay, okay, Max, I'm up!" she said, and got out of bed. "I guess I have to get ready to walk all the other dogs anyway."

Before long CJ was kneeling on the floor to snap the leash onto my collar. "Wow, Max, you've been growing!" she said, and fiddled with the collar so that it was a bit looser around my neck. It felt better, and I shook my head energetically, hearing the tag jangle.

"That's a little loose," CJ said, frowning. "Well, you'll grow into it, I guess. Okay, okay, let's go!" In half a minute she and I were out the door. "No, Sneakers, sorry!" she said, shutting the door in the cat's face.

This time we didn't just head straight outside. Instead, CJ took me down to the floor below and knocked on a door. When it opened, Duke was on the other side waiting for us, whining a little with happiness.

He put his giant nose down to mine and licked my face with enough force that I nearly tumbled over onto my side. I jumped back up and barked at him to let him know that I was still in charge. Then I licked his nose back.

Duke's owner laughed. "He's calmed down a little, hasn't he?" she asked CJ.

"Just a little," CJ agreed, and took Duke's leash in her hand.

"I saw all your posters," Duke's owner said as I tugged on my own leash, ready to get outside. "Do you have an extra one? I'll put it up at work."

CJ tugged a folded square of paper out of her pocket. "Thanks," she said, and finally she paid attention to what I was trying to tell her, that it was time to go. We headed downstairs and out into the street.

We stopped at two other apartment buildings to pick up Honey and Jay, and then I took my position where I belonged, at the head of the pack, leading us all to the dog park. We paused at a corner, waiting on the curb as cars whizzed back and forth. I was quivering a little with impatience, ready to run, to wrestle, to find a ball and defend it from any other dog who wanted to get his teeth into it.

There were feet on all sides—feet in boots, feet in sandals, some in sneakers like CJ's, some in high heels like Jillian's. When all the feet started to move off the curb, I moved with them, tugging CJ into the street. Why wait?

CJ, close on my heels with all the other dogs, laughed a little. "So that's how you do it!" she said. "You're showing me how to live in New York, Max!"

Her voice made my tail wag harder, but I didn't slow down or turn around. We were almost there!

The dog park near the apartment wasn't as big as the park a few days ago, where we had met Stella. And there weren't as many dogs. But that was good in a way, because it meant I didn't have to spend as much time teaching other dogs to respect me. It didn't take them long to learn that I was Max. Nobody tried to take my ball away (even if all I could do was gnaw on it). Everyone figured out that I was supposed to win when we wrestled.

Duke stayed close behind me, and lots of the other owners laughed to see us together. "Are those both yours?" some of them asked CJ.

"No, I'm just walking Duke. He's the Great Dane. And Max—the little one—he needs a home," CJ would say back. "Soon. By Tuesday. It's really important. Could you ask around? Can you put a poster up, maybe?"

She handed out her papers and stuck a few on the trees with brightly colored little tacks. It was odd how humans—even CJ—seemed to like papers so much, even more than balls or sticks. But that's just the way they are. Maybe one day they'll learn more about how to have fun.

After a while I got tired of teaching the other dogs how to behave and returned to CJ, who was sitting on a bench with a sketch pad on her knee. She put her pencil and paper down to pick me up and put me on her lap. It felt good to be high up, eye to eye with the other dogs for once, keeping watch over everything going on. Duke sat beside us and put his head on the bench. He knew not to lay it in CJ's lap while I was there.

Jay finished running in his last big circle and came panting to CJ's side. She called to Honey, who was resting beneath another bench, and then clipped all of our leashes on. I jumped up to lead us back home, and we were walking along one of the paths in the park when I smelled something that I recognized.

Dogs. People who seemed familiar. Antiseptic soap and dog food and chilly cement. The smell reminded me of the shelter, and I left my place at the head of my pack to move a little closer to CJ.

CJ slowed down and came to a stop as well, holding all four leashes.

Across a little lawn, I could see pens with puppies and older dogs in them. I could see people stopping to look. Children were begging to pet the dogs. Grown-ups were admiring the furry little things. A tall woman with curly brown hair walked back and forth, talking, picking up puppies to put them into waiting hands, handing out papers.

Her smell drifted to me faintly. It was Gail.

CJ sighed. She pulled at our leashes and took us down a different path, away from the pens and the dogs and Gail. I wasn't quite sure why, but I was glad she did so. I wasn't nobody's dog anymore. I lived with CJ now, and that was how things should be.

"Three more days," CJ muttered under her breath as we walked.

We returned Honey and Jay to their apartments and then CJ and Duke and I headed back to Jillian's. My legs were getting a little tired from pushing myself to stay in front of the big dogs, and I was starting to think that it would be nice to curl up on CJ's quilt for a rest.

As we came closer to the apartment building, I heard something that made my ears perk up. Barking. Angry, ferocious barking. It got louder the closer we approached.

CJ went tense. Even Duke looked interested.

The barking was coming from an alley that ran

alongside the apartment building. I strained at the leash, pulling CJ toward the source of all that noise.

"Max, no. We better not," she said.

I was starting to understand that word, "no." I didn't like it. I pulled harder.

"Max!" CJ said sternly. Duke looked at her to see if he was in trouble.

Then we heard a new noise—a cat's yowl. It was furious and frightened all at once, and it rose from a low grumble to a high shriek.

CJ gasped. I dragged her two more steps forward. Now I could see around the corner of the alley.

I could see Baxter.

He was halfway down the alley with his rump toward us. Crouched in front of him was a gray cat with a smell I knew very well.

"Sneakers!" CJ shouted.

13

Sneakers was crouched low to the ground with her ears flat against her head and her mouth open as wide as it could go, showing all of her sharp white teeth. She was wagging her tail and her fur bristled all over so that she'd look as big as possible to Baxter.

One slim gray paw shot out and whacked Baxter right on the nose. I remembered how sharp those claws were! And now I realized that, when Sneakers had smacked me in the face a few days ago, it had just been a warning, not really meant to hurt. When she was dealing with Baxter, however, she had other intentions.

Baxter was so startled that a bark cut off halfway through, and he jumped back a little. Then he crouched low and growled, a long, low, deadly threat.

I could smell Sneakers's fear, even over the rage and aggression that were wafting off Baxter. He was furious that such a little scrap of an animal got to exist near his home, and he was going to do something about it.

And I was going to do something about *him*.

Both times I'd met Baxter, CJ had picked me up so that I never got a chance to show him who was boss. Now was the moment! I lunged forward with all the strength in my body, but my leash yanked me back.

"Max, no!" CJ screamed. "Max, stay!"

I knew she was talking to me, but I didn't know what she meant. And it didn't matter, not at that moment. I'd go back to being CJ's dog in a minute, but first I needed to teach Baxter exactly who was in charge in this alley.

I shook my head and twisted sideways, pulling against the leash, and to my delight my collar slipped off right over my head. CJ gasped in horror and lunged to grab me, but I dodged her reaching hands and shot as fast as I could straight at Baxter.

The big dog didn't even turn to notice me! That

wouldn't do at all. I couldn't teach him that I was the leader if he ignored me.

I nipped his back foot hard. Mid-bark, he whirled to face me.

His face loomed above me, and bubbles of saliva frothed among his strong white teeth. A few lines, marked with beads of blood, showed up along the shiny black surface of his nose.

I leaped up as high as I could and nipped his nose, right where the red lines were. It wasn't that hard a bite—I only wanted to teach him, not hurt him. But he jumped back with a yelp of pain, and that's when a small gray form darted past us both. Sneakers raced for the mouth of the alley, where CJ was still standing with my leash dangling from her hand.

Jillian was next to her. I wondered when she'd gotten here, but I didn't have much time to think of it. I wasn't done with Baxter.

CJ was shouting at Baxter to get back, to get away, that he was a bad, bad dog. And it was true! He was! I growled as loudly as I could, dropping my head low to the ground. I stepped forward one pace, then two. If Baxter knew what was good for him, he'd go away.

And he did. Still growling, shaking his head resentfully, he backed up a few paces down the alley. I stopped advancing and stood still, letting him know that he could stay there, but he shouldn't come any farther toward me.

"Baxter!" yelled a new voice. "There you are!"

Baxter's owner came running along the alley toward his dog, swinging a leash in his hand. I turned my head to take a quick look back at CJ. I knew she was upset and frightened; I'd been able to hear it in her voice. I could take care of her now.

Duke was standing between me and CJ. He was right behind me, as he'd been all morning at the dog park. With my attention fixed on Baxter, I hadn't even noticed he was there.

The Great Dane put his nose down to sniff me, and I sniffed back. Then I walked between his stilt-like legs, right under his belly, to where CJ was running to scoop me up. She grabbed Duke's leash, too, pulling him away from Baxter.

Jillian had picked up Sneakers and was holding the cat in her arms. Sneakers seemed to be holding her, too. All four of her legs were spread wide to cling to Jillian, and her claws were out so she could grip her tightly.

Jillian's face was very white. CJ's, too. I could feel

CJ trembling a little. But it was all right now, and I hoped she'd realize it soon. I'd taken care of everything.

"Hey, your cat scratched up my dog!" Baxter's owner said, striding down the alley toward us with Baxter on his leash.

"My cat? My *cat*? My cat scratched your *dog*?" Jillian demanded.

She had a lot more to say, with words like "lawyer" and "Animal Control" and "co-op board" and "eviction," but CJ and Duke and I didn't stay around to listen. CJ pulled on our leashes and got us inside, which was too bad—I was ready to teach Baxter his manners again. With his owner at his side, he seemed to have found his courage once more, and he was growling.

Some dogs need a lot of lessons, and it looked like Baxter was one of them.

CJ delivered Duke to his apartment and talked to the owner there for a little while. Then we both went back home. She collapsed on the couch, holding me tightly, until I squirmed in her arms to remind her that snuggling was all very well and good, but I needed to breathe as well.

She was still trembling, though, so I licked her ear and cheek and as much of her face as I could manage, trying to tell her that she never had to worry about dogs like Baxter, not when I was there to protect her. And I'd always be there to protect her. I was meant to be her dog.

The door opened and Jillian came in, with Sneakers still in her arms. She stood still for a moment or two, looking at us, and then came and sat down on the couch next to us.

Sneakers shook herself out of Jillian's hands, leaped off the couch, found a spot of carpet that she liked, and began to wash herself all over.

"Don't worry," said Jillian. "I'm reporting that jerk to the co-op board. Either that dog will be out of here, or he will."

CJ nodded.

"That little dog . . ." Jillian said.

CJ wiped at her face. "Max," she said.

Jillian nodded. "He ran right at that horrible beast. I couldn't believe it. I've never seen a dog as brave as that."

CJ hugged me. "I know. Max is the toughest dog I ever met."

"You have to be tough to make it in New York," Jillian said. "And I guess I'd be pretty ungrateful if I said he couldn't stay, wouldn't I?"

CJ sat up straight, and some of her fear and worry

fell right away. I could feel it. I must have done a good job of comforting her.

"You mean it?" she asked Jillian.

"I don't say things I don't mean," Jillian said. She looked at me thoughtfully and put her hand out toward my face.

"Gentle, Max," CJ told me.

I looked around for a treat. Jillian tentatively rubbed behind my ears.

"I don't really know much about dogs," she said. "But I have to admit it—New York is where this one belongs."

I took us all to the dog park again the next day, and the day after that it was one of those mornings when CJ had to pack her backpack and rush away. Jillian was home, though, tapping away on her flat plastic tray, and she even took me out to pee halfway through the morning.

I would rather it had been CJ, but I made the best of it.

CJ came home in the afternoon, and Stella was with her. Today Stella had on sandals that laced all the way up to her knees. The girls said hello to Jillian and got my leash, clipping it onto the brand-new collar that Jillian had bought for me. Then I took them both outside for a good long walk.

CJ and Stella were busy with the papers again, tearing them down from walls and signposts and trees. It was a strange game, but if it made them happy, I didn't mind.

And CJ was happy. I could see it in her face and hear it in her voice and feel it coming off her body in waves.

"But you know, if Jillian hadn't changed her mind, the posters would have worked," Stella said.

"I know. I actually got a call this morning and had to tell him Max already found a home," CJ said.

"Plus someone from my mom's work was interested, too," Stella added. "She said, 'Who could resist the adorable little face in that drawing?' I *said* you were good at drawing animals! No way, don't blush like that. I heard the teacher tell you this morning how good that sketch of Sneakers and Max is. And you know what? Jenna heard, too. Did you see her practically turn green?"

They laughed together as CJ pulled down another paper, crumpled it up, and tossed it into a trash can. Then Stella stopped by the side of the street and waved her hand at the passing traffic.

"See, that thing on the top of the cab, with the

numbers?" she said to CJ. "You have to look for one where the numbers are lit up. Like that one!" She waved wildly and a yellow car came swerving out of the traffic to stop by the curb, right in front of her.

Stella reached for the handle of the back door, but before she could get her hand on it, a man who'd been walking down the sidewalk cut right in front of her. He had a dark suit on and a briefcase in one hand, and he pulled the door open.

"Hey, that's our cab!" Stella said indignantly.

The man ignored her. "Downtown, Columbus Circle, and I'm in a hurry!" he said to the driver of the car.

"We can get another one, Stella," CJ muttered.

But I was interested in the inside of the cab. It smelled intriguing. Lots of people had been there, sitting on the seat, and some of them had been eating food.

I jumped forward, and my leash slipped out of CJ's hand as I dodged around the man with the briefcase and leaped up into the car. After a short scramble, I was up on the seat.

The man was still standing by the door of the cab, looking stunned. He was in between me and my girl, and I didn't like the way he was standing.

I lifted my lip from my teeth, just to show him I meant business. Nobody had told me to be Gentle, Max right then.

"Hey, get that dog out of there!" the man said, turning to CJ.

Stella ducked around him and sat on the seat beside me, sliding over to make room for CJ. "Good dog, Max!" she said, so I let her. "Come on, CJ!"

"I've got an important meeting!" the man said angrily.

"I've got an important dog!" CJ said, and she ducked past him, too, and sat down on the seat of the car so that I was between her and Stella. Stella leaned over both of us to grab the door handle and slam the door shut.

In the seat ahead of us, the cabdriver was shaking his head and laughing. "I don't usually let dogs in here, but I'll make an exception for that one," he said. "I'm afraid he'll chew my arm off if I don't! Where are you girls headed?"

"The Brooklyn Bridge!" said Stella. "We're going to walk across. My friend needs to see the sights. And her dog, too!"

I settled myself on CJ's lap and propped my front feet up against the window as the car moved out into the traffic. CJ put the window down a little for me so that I could get my nose up to the crack and sniff as hard as I could.

Air rushed into my nose, packed with all the delicious city smells. I wasn't sure where we were headed, but it was going to be wonderful.

There was a lot of this city left to explore, and I was ready to lead the way.

O ver the next few weeks I got used to the idea that CJ would leave me alone in the mornings. Jillian usually took me out at least once, and after that I'd rest or sniff around the apartment or sometimes curl up with Sneakers until my girl came back.

Then we'd go out. I *loved* going out with CJ. Sometimes Stella would come with us. We walked all over the sidewalks, and went to a lot of parks and in a few more cars. I got used to being tucked into CJ's bag when we'd go down the steps and ride in the rattling, swaying subway.

Then, one morning, CJ didn't pack up her backpack full of her papers. But she didn't take me out so that I could lead our pack to the dog park either. That was strange.

Instead, CJ stayed in her room, pulling shirts and

pants and T-shirts out of a dresser, shaking them out and folding them. A blue T-shirt slipped out of her hands and landed at my feet. I loved the smell of CJ's clothes, so I seized the T-shirt in my teeth and gave it a good shake.

"No, Max, I need that!" CJ said, reaching down.

A game of tug-of-war with my girl! Excellent! I pulled back on the T-shirt and let CJ tug me about the room. "No, Max!" she said again, but she was laughing. I had learned that "No, Max!" did not mean anything bad when CJ was laughing, so I braced my feet on the rug and pulled harder.

CJ groaned. "Max, really," she said. Now she wasn't laughing, so I stopped pulling and cocked my head to look up at her. She twitched the T-shirt out of my mouth and put it in the suitcase that she had open on the bed.

I was interested in that suitcase. It had all of CJ's attention, which was obviously wrong. I was her dog, and she was supposed to be paying attention to me! I put my front paws up on the bed and whined and barked a few times, until CJ gave in and picked me up.

"Okay, but just for a few seconds," CJ said.

She set me on the bed and I poked my nose into the suitcase, which I liked very much. It was full of CJ's clothes and smelled like CJ.

"All packed?" asked a voice from the doorway.

Jillian stood there, leaning on the doorframe and looking in.

"Almost," CJ said.

Jillian nodded and walked into the room. "What about all this stuff?" she said, stopping at the desk.

The desk was covered with CJ's papers and paints and pencils. "I'm going to put that away next," CJ said.

Jillian stood still, looking down at the desk. "Hmmm. This one, too?" she asked.

CJ turned away from the suitcase to look at the paper that Jillian had picked up. I took the opportunity to jump into the suitcase and burrow under a gray sweatshirt. I loved how soft it was, all over my body, and how much it smelled like my girl.

"Oh, that's a good one," CJ said to Jillian. "One of my best. I made a sketch of Max and Sneakers sleeping all curled up like that, and I finished it in watercolors at the school."

"Yes, it's a good one," said Jillian. "How much?"

"What?" CJ asked. She sounded shocked.

I stuck my head out from under the sweatshirt to see if my girl needed me. But nothing seemed to be dangerous, so I burrowed back under the sweatshirt. A sock was right under my nose, and it had not been washed since the last time CJ wore it. It was delectably smelly. I chewed on it contentedly.

"How much?" I heard Jillian say again. "For the painting. You're an artist, right? Artists sell their work. How much would you sell that painting for?"

"Uh . . ." CJ sounded as if she had no idea what to say. "Jillian, I mean . . . you've been so nice, letting me stay here and all. And letting Max stay, too. If you want the painting . . ."

"No way. Don't do that." Jillian shook her head. "You did work, right? Work should be paid for. You didn't walk those dogs all summer for free. You don't do art for free, either. How does two hundred dollars sound?"

"Two hundred dollars!" CJ gasped. "Jillian, I can't take that!"

"Then I can't take the painting. Which is a shame, because I really want it."

"Oh. Well. I . . . I just . . ."

"It's a deal, then?"

"Um. I guess. It's a deal."

"Good. Here you go. I'm going to put it on the mantelpiece for now, and get it framed later. We'd better leave in about half an hour if we want to beat the traffic over the bridge."

"Okay. Okay. Thanks, Jillian." I could hear in CJ's voice that she was smiling. "Thanks. For everything."

CJ came back over to the suitcase. "Two hundred dollars, Max! Can you believe it?" she asked. "Max? Max, where did you go?"

I heard my name, and I poked my head up to reassure my girl that I was here to take care of her. But the sweatshirt still covered me completely. I shook my head hard, but I couldn't get the sweatshirt off.

Then CJ plucked the soft gray cloth off my head. She stood looking down at me with the sweatshirt in one hand and several small slips of paper clutched in the other.

With her sock still in my mouth, I looked up and wagged. Maybe we'd play some more tug-of-war.

"Oh, Max!" CJ groaned.

14

After all of our fun games with her clothes and the suitcase, I could not understand at all what CJ did next. She shut me in a pen, just like the people at the shelter used to do! Except that this pen was smaller and made of plastic, with only one tiny opening in front, covered with wire mesh.

Then she did something even stranger. She picked up the pen and carried it!

The whole thing rocked and swung in her hand, and I braced my legs on the slippery plastic floor, trying to keep myself from sliding. I barked, trying to let her know what a ridiculous mistake she had made, locking me in here.

"I know, Max, I know," she said. "Don't worry, it's not for long."

But she didn't let me out.

CJ put me, still in the pen, inside the back of a car. That made me remember traveling from the shelter to the park where I had finally found CJ and turned her into my girl.

And I started to worry.

Worrying was not something I was used to doing. I was Max! I knew how to be Gentle, Max when CJ wanted me to be, but I could also teach humans and even dogs like Baxter to respect me. I didn't have to worry. I could take care of myself, and my girl, too.

But I did not care for the way the car hummed and vibrated as it started up. This was not like riding in cabs, on CJ's lap. I was locked away, far from my girl, and the unsettling feeling of moving in a way I didn't choose, to a place I couldn't even see, made me start to feel like that tiny puppy again. The last time I'd been in a vehicle that moved like this, I'd been separated from my mother and my sisters.

That had turned out all right, because I'd found CJ. But what was happening now? Would there be another separation coming? Would something take me away from my girl?

I *hated* that idea. I barked. When that didn't work, I growled.

When that didn't work, I whined.

"Oh, Max!" I heard CJ say. "I had no idea he'd hate the car so much. He didn't mind riding in cabs. I guess it's being in the carrier. It's okay, Max, sweetie. You'll be out soon."

But even her voice didn't truly help. Nothing helped. I needed to be in her lap, to feel her hands on my fur, to lick her face and sniff her scent and know that she was always going to be my girl. Until that happened, I could not stop complaining.

At last—at *last!*—the car pulled to a stop. I heard something bang. Then CJ lifted my pen out of the back and unlocked the door.

Trembling, I leaped out and threw myself on her. "Shh, Max, shh, it's okay," she soothed, holding me in her arms, stroking me from my ears to my tail. "It's all over now. We're home."

I didn't understand what she was saying, and I didn't care too much. I was so relieved to be in her arms again that I just cuddled against her and sighed.

She carried me around the car. We were outside a building much smaller than Jillian's apartment building. Jillian had gotten out of the car as well and was standing and talking to a tall woman in a flowery blouse. This new woman looked confused and kept staring at me and CJ, wide-eyed.

CJ put her chin up slightly and straightened her back.

"Clarity June, what is *that*?" the new woman said.

"This is Max," CJ said. "He's mine."

I wagged a little when I heard my name. I was starting to feel better.

The new woman said a lot of words in a high-pitched voice that I did not care for. I picked up my head from where it lay in the crook of CJ's neck and looked around.

The building we were all standing next to had only two stories. It seemed surprisingly small. I could smell that the woman in the flowery blouse lived here, and there was even a smell of CJ! It was old and faint, but I could still tell that this was a place where CJ had spent a lot of time.

And there was another smell, too.

A dog. Female. Older than me, but not as old as Honey. She hadn't been here lately; the smells were not fresh. But like CJ, she had spent a lot of time here.

My ears pricked up. My spine stiffened. I squirmed to let CJ know to let me down. When she set me on the grass, I got to work, sniffing hard, trying to figure out where this other dog had gone.

"He needed me, and I kept him, Gloria," CJ said firmly. "I didn't have a choice. I'll take care of him just like I take care of Molly. You won't even notice he's around."

"Well, you might notice," Jillian murmured.

"Clarity June, I don't know what's come over you," the new woman fussed. "It's like you go away to the city for the summer and you come back a completely new person."

Just then the breeze brought a scent to my nose. The dog who used to live here—she was nearby!

I jerked my head around. A figure turned the corner—a tall, lanky boy, walking a dog on a leash. The dog was straining forward, pulling him until he had to trot. CJ laughed. "Molly!" she called out. "Oh no, Trent, don't let her go—she has to meet Max!"

But the boy had already released his grip on the dog's leash.

She raced forward, panting, and threw herself at CJ. CJ dropped to her knees to hug this new dog and let her face be covered with kisses.

I sat back on my haunches in astonishment. This dog was licking my girl. Getting petted by my girl. Getting hugged by my girl!

"Oh, Molly, Molly, I missed you, too!" CJ crooned.

She had both arms full of happy, squirming, wagging dog. "Trent, grab Max!" she called. "Gentle, Max!"

The boy who had been walking the other dog ran up and dropped down beside me to take hold of my collar. I would have shown him that it wasn't okay to grab at me like that, but I was too riveted by the sight of CJ with another dog. Besides, CJ had told me to be gentle.

I had seen CJ with other dogs before. With Duke and Jay and Honey. She'd pet them and scratch them and talk to them, but they never got all her attention the way I did. I was her dog, and the others were just friends.

CJ set Molly down gently by her side and then both turned a little to face me. Molly sat inside the circle of CJ's arm, panting with happiness, her tongue lolling out of her mouth, her black eyes bright and joyful. She wasn't challenging me, exactly, so I wasn't sure how to show her that I was meant to be in charge. She hardly looked at me. All her excitement— all her attention—all her love—was for CJ.

And CJ adored Molly. I could feel the love coming off my girl in waves.

That was . . . interesting.

"Look at Max," CJ marveled. "He's being so good!"

I was glad she'd looked up at me, remembered

that I was more important. I was glad when she held out her hand and I shook my collar loose from the boy's grasp and went to her.

The other dog, Molly, looked away from CJ long enough to touch noses with me. I could smell my girl on her.

That made it hard to growl at her or raise my hackles or show her my teeth.

There didn't seem to be anything else to do but cuddle under CJ's free arm and nuzzle my head into her side. If CJ wanted another dog around, I supposed I could get used to it. I'd gotten used to Sneakers, after all. Another dog should be easy after that.

As long as Molly always remembered that I was the boss. After all, I was Max.

STARSCAPE BOOKS
Reading & Activity Guide to

Max's Story:
A Dog's Purpose
Puppy Tale
By W. Bruce Cameron

Ages 8–12; Grades 3–7

Max's Story: A Dog's Purpose Puppy Tale introduces readers to Max, a spunky Chihuahua–Yorkshire Terrier (Yorkie) mixed-breed puppy with a big personality and an even bigger heart. Written from Max's perspective, the story follows the spirited pup's journey from a dog shelter into the life and heart of CJ, a young girl struggling to feel at home in bustling New York City, where she's attending a special art program for the summer. As they "train each other" to be a good owner and pet, respectively, CJ and Max also teach each other important lessons about how to bridge the sometimes confusing gap between how you see the world and how the world sees you. (CJ is also a key character in W. Bruce Cameron's *Molly's Story: A Dog's Purpose Puppy Tale.* If you have read, or have an opportunity to read, that story as well, you might enjoy comparing CJ's experiences with Molly to her adventures with Max.)

Reading *Max's Story: A Dog's Purpose Puppy Tale* with Your Children

Pre-Reading Discussion Questions

1. The central relationship in *Max's Story: A Dog's Purpose Puppy Tale* is between a puppy and a person. Do you have a special relationship with a pet in your life, or can you imagine what it might be like if you did? Usually, we think of a person training, or teaching, a pet. In this story, a young girl named CJ learns a lot from a small puppy. Can you think of something you learned from an experience with your own pet, a friend's pet, a class pet, or from reading a story, or watching a movie, about a special animal?

2. In this story, the *human* main character, CJ, hopes to be an artist. In order to attend a special art program, she has to live away from home for the summer, be apart from another beloved pet (her dog back home, Molly), and get used to life in a big city. Do you have a dream, or goal, that you are working toward in school, sports, the arts, or another area? Do you have to make

sacrifices, or face challenges, like CJ does, to pursue *your* dream?

Post-Reading Discussion Questions

1. *Max's Story: A Dog's Purpose Puppy Tale* is told entirely from Max's perspective. Max doesn't understand human language, but he manages to successfully "translate," or interpret, at least parts of people's conversations. What "cues" does he use to do this?

2. At first, Max perceives Gail and the other shelter workers and puppies as "giants." But eventually he realizes that is not the case. In Chapter 1, he thinks: "And that's when I realized an important truth. All of the dogs around me and the women who took care of us—they weren't big. It was the other way around. *I* was small!" How does this realization affect Max? How does it influence the way he acts toward people and other dogs? How does Max's view of himself differ from how his caretakers view him?

3. How does Max take matters into his own paws at the second adoption event to get to CJ and alert her that she "made a mistake" to leave without him? What are some of the physical obstacles Max encounters in getting to CJ? What are

some of the personal challenges CJ has to consider before agreeing to adopt Max?

4. In Chapter 4, Gail, the shelter worker, tells CJ: "Dogs sometimes choose their people. We don't know how they know, but they just *know*. And that's what I think has happened with you and Max." Do you agree with Gail? Do you think animals choose their people, or people choose their animals? Why do you think Max is drawn to CJ? In what ways do they both have to act bigger, or braver, than they actually are, or feel?

5. How does CJ's mother's friend Jillian (who CJ is staying with for the summer) react to Max's arrival? How does Jillian's cat (Sneakers) react? How does the relationship between Max and Sneakers evolve, or change, over the course of the story? Do you think two pets, like Max and Sneakers, can become "friends"? Why or why not?

6. In Chapter 5, Max says: "That was one of my jobs, keeping my girl happy. And the other was to protect her from anything that might hurt her." Max's sense of purpose is the driving force behind many of his feelings and actions. Can you cite some examples from the story that illustrate how Max fulfills his purpose? What are

some of the things he does to make CJ happy? What are some of the things he does to keep her safe?

7. In Chapter 6, as she struggles with a drawing, CJ worries aloud to Max that she's not talented enough to succeed in her art program. Then Jillian enters. What do we learn about CJ from the conversation that follows? What kind of relationship does CJ seem to have with her mother? What does Jillian think about CJ's art program? How does CJ feel about being in New York City?

8. How does having Max help CJ develop her friendship with Stella? What do you think Stella means when she says Max is "a New York dog" in Chapter 8? How does Max's toughness and curiosity inspire CJ's discovery of her own "survival skills" for city living?

9. What are the naughty things Max and Sneakers do, in Chapters 8 and 9, which lead Jillian to change her mind about allowing CJ to keep Max? How much time does she give CJ to find Max a new home?

10. In Chapter 11, CJ says: "I needed Molly so much, Max. I was younger when I got her, and stuff at home . . . it wasn't so great. But you—it's different with you. You need *me*." Do you agree with

CJ's perspective, that Max needs her? Or do you agree with Max's belief that CJ needs him? Can both be correct? Can an animal and a person "rescue each other"?

11. What does Max do when he sees Sneakers trapped by the mean dog, Baxter, in the alley near Jillian's apartment? Do you think Max does the right thing when he disobeys CJ's command to "stay"? Why do you think Max notes: "I'd go back to being CJ's dog in a minute, but first I needed to teach Baxter exactly who was in charge in this alley." Is Max the only "hero" in Sneakers's rescue? What role does Duke, the Great Dane, play? How does the incident with Baxter and Sneakers change Jillian's view of Max? How does Jillian's behavior toward Max change?

12. In Chapter 13, CJ hesitates at first, but then tells a man who is trying to cut Stella, CJ, and Max off from a cab Stella had called over for them: "I've got an important dog!" How does CJ's choice to get into the cab and make this bold statement demonstrate how her attitude has changed? How has Max's conviction that *he* is important helped CJ to realize *her own* value and importance?

13. In the last chapter, CJ's mother, Gloria, com-

ments that CJ has come back from her summer in the city "a completely new person." Do you think she means it as a compliment or an insult? Why?

14. How does Max react to CJ's friend, Trent? What does Max think of CJ's *other* dog, Molly? Do you get the sense that Max will be able to form a new "pack" that includes Trent and Molly? Do you think you will see dogs differently, now that you've read *Max's Story: A Dog's Purpose Puppy Tale*?

Post-Reading Activities

Take the story from the page to the pavement with these fun and inspiring activities for the dog lovers in your family.

1. THE DOG'S-EYE VIEW AND YOURS, TOO. All the characters, scenes, and events in this story are presented from Max's puppy perspective. How might a *person's* description, or perception, of some of these things be different from Max's? Invite your child to choose a person, place, or event from the story (CJ; Jillian's apartment; or a dog-walking outing, for example) and describe it to you in his or her own words. Together, discuss the similarities and differences

between Max's and your child's descriptions. Discuss how size, eye level, knowledge of language, sharpness of senses, priorities, and purpose might influence the descriptions.

2. ART FROM THE HEART. At one point in the story, CJ is second-guessing her artistic ability. She feels disappointed when the instructor calls one of her drawings "inauthentic," suggesting something about it doesn't "ring true," or the work feels forced or artificial. When CJ focuses on subjects she feels passionate about, and can closely relate to, like her beloved Max, or the black Lab playing with "his boy" in Central Park, her artwork improves. Invite your child to think about a pet, person, or place he or she feels passionate about, and encourage them to do a drawing, painting, or modeling-clay sculpture. Gather supplies, such as colored pencils, erasers, markers, brushes, paint, and paper. Perhaps you can invite other family members or friends to do pieces as well. You might even mount pictures on poster board and display sculptures in an "art show" for family, friends, or neighbors to enjoy.

3. HOW CAN YOU HELP? In the story, Gail and the shelter workers are working hard to help

homeless puppies like Max. As Gail explains to CJ, shelters don't have an endless supply of resources. You and your child might host a "Lend a Paw a Hand" Party, to bring a group of friends and family members together to make pet-safe items to donate to the shelter. Look online to find instructions for easy-to-make pet-safe toys and treats. Print out directions and recipes. Invite guests to bring felt or fleece scraps, recyclable plastic bottles, and other found items from around their homes. You and your child can deliver the "goodies" to the shelter. If possible, ask a shelter staff member if they can email some pictures of pets enjoying the goodies for you to share with the folks who helped make them.

Reading *Max's Story: A Dog's Purpose Puppy Tale* in Your Classroom

These Common Core–aligned writing activities may be used in conjunction with the pre- and post-reading discussion questions above.

1. **Point of View:** Max, the feisty Chihuahua-Yorkie protagonist and narrator of *Max's Story: A Dog's Purpose Puppy Tale*, encounters Sneakers

the cat, at the apartment where "his girl" CJ is spending the summer. Max is bewildered by Sneakers's decidedly non-canine ways. But what does *Sneakers* think of Max? What does sharing "her" apartment with a rambunctious newcomer look like from Sneakers's perspective? Have students write two to three paragraphs from Sneakers's point of view. Use the humorous and compelling voice the author created for Max as a model. Take special note of the unique details, sensory-driven descriptions, and reinforcement of key character traits that the author used to lend Max's voice authenticity.

2. **Communities and Relationships:** Although she is surrounded by a city full of people and possibilities, CJ feels lonely and disconnected in New York City. With Max's help, CJ cultivates a friendship with Stella, and explores more of New York City. Through her dog-walking job and excursions to dog-friendly Central Park, CJ discovers a fluid, but friendly, "canine community" of dogs and dog lovers, which reveals a "softer," more playful side of New York City and New Yorkers. If CJ had known about all of this before she arrived in New York City, she probably would have had a more comfortable transi-

tion to her summer "home." Have students write a series of "welcome postcards" to CJ. Include postcards from Jillian, CJ's art teacher, Gail (the shelter worker), Stella, and, of course, Max. Using details from the novel and your imagination, think about what each of these "pen pals" might tell CJ, to get her excited about her upcoming summer in NYC.

3. **Text Type: Opinion Piece.** In the story, Max makes humorous observations about how humans use, or perhaps overuse, technology. He thinks CJ and Jillian should spend less time with cell phones and computers, and more time with dogs like him. There is a saying that there can be "truth in humor." Do you think Max has a point? Do you think technology sometimes takes up too much time in people's lives today? Write a one-page essay explaining why you agree or disagree with Max on this point.

4. **Text Type: Narrative.** In the character of Jillian, write the story of your summer with CJ and Max. How did your positive (and negative) experiences with them affect your view of dogs in general and Max in particular? How did your opinion of CJ's artistic potential change? What did you learn about bravery and loyalty from

Max and CJ's relationship, or from the bond that developed between Max and your own cat, Sneakers? Is what you gained from CJ and Max a "fair trade" for the inconvenience they sometimes caused in your life and home?

5. **Research & Present: FOSTERING PETS IN NEED.** In *Max's Story: A Dog's Purpose Puppy Tale*, Gail and the shelter workers are trying to find people to adopt Max and other homeless puppies. Fostering, or caring for a pet in your home for a designated time, is another important way people can help dogs and other pets in need. Go to the library or online to learn more about fostering, or your local shelter's foster program. (HINT: Visit https:www.paws.org/get -involved/foster/ for a helpful overview of fostering, and to check out an example of a foster program in action.) Use your research to create an informative booklet about fostering programs and opportunities. If possible, make copies to share with classmates, friends, and other members of your school community.

6. **Research & Present: WHICH BREED DO YOU NEED?** In *Max's Story: A Dog's Purpose Puppy Tale*, CJ walks dogs of different breeds, with different personalities. CJ's special relation-

ship with Max illustrates that some dogs, or dog breeds, are only "a good fit" for particular owners or situations. Go to the library or online to learn more about different breeds. (Hint: Visit www.akc.org.) Reaching out to local vets or breeders might be helpful, too. Select two to three breeds you find interesting. Find out about their personalities, energy levels space and exercise requirements, grooming needs, and health issues. Use your research to create a PowerPoint or other multimedia style presentation to share with your classmates. Include your recommendations for the kinds of owners or environments you'd recommend for each of the breeds.

Supports English Language Arts Common Core Writing Standards: W.3.1, 3.2, 3.3, 3.7; W.4.1, 4.2, 4.3, 4.7; W.5.1, 5.2, 5.3, 5.7; W.6.2, 6.3, 6.7; W.7.2, 7.3, 7.7

About the Author

W. BRUCE CAMERON is the *New York Times* best-selling author of *A Dog's Purpose, A Dog's Journey,* and *The Dogs of Christmas*. His books for young readers include *Ellie's Story: A Dog's Purpose Puppy Tale, Bailey's Story: A Dog's Purpose Puppy Tale,* and *Molly's Story: A Dog's Purpose Puppy Tale*. He lives in California.